Staring Up at the Sun

Staring up at the Sun

Suzanne Bugler

Hodder
Children's
Books

a division of Hodder Headline Limited

A Catalogue record for this book is available from the British Library

ISBN-10: 0 340 90227 2

Typeset in Goudy Old Style by Avon DataSet Ltd,
Bidford-on-Avon, Warwickshire

Printed and bound in Great Britain by
Bookmarque Ltd, Croydon, Surrey

The paper and board used in this paperback by Hodder Children's Books
are natural recyclable products made from wood grown in
sustainable forests. The manufacturing processes conform to the
environmental regulations of the country of origin.

Hodder Children's Books
A division of Hodder Headline Limited
338 Euston Road
London NW1 3BH

To Nick

1

Sara came to our school two weeks after we started in Year Ten. She stood at the front of the class and stared at her feet while Mrs Rupert droned on about how welcome we had to make her feel. Sara didn't wear shoes, she wore dirty old trainers with the laces half-undone and old off-white nylon socks, rolled right down so they looked like ankle socks. They weren't even decent trainers; we all noticed that. They were bulky, nylon things, like you get on the bottom rack of chain stores.

I lolled over my desk, looking at her. September sun streamed through the window on to my back. It was only just after nine but already the heat through the glass was killing. We were still just wearing our summer polo tops but Sara had a black V-neck jumper on over hers, like the boys wore and we'd worn too in the first year till we'd gone over to cardigans. Juliet nudged me and slipped a piece of paper under my hand. She'd written *MINGER* on it and she giggled when I read it, clamping her hand over her mouth so it came out in a half-stifled snort.

Sara's head snapped up and her eyes narrowed on

Juliet, and then on me. They were green eyes. The sun caught them and they glinted like a witch's. I held her stare, mesmerized.

'She'll be with most of you for English and Maths and PE,' Mrs Rupert said, while Sara stood there scowling at us, mean eyes clocking it all, 'and with you, Kate, for Art and Biology. So if you'd care to move along a bit you can make a space for her now and show her the way to the Art block after tutorial. I expect you girls to look after her.'

She didn't much look like she needed looking after. I shuffled along a bit, moving closer to Juliet, and Mrs Rupert dragged a spare chair over and put it next to me on the other side. Sara plonked herself on to the chair, and threw her bag down on to the desk in front of her and started tugging at a thread in a tear in the canvas. It was an old army surplus bag, a sort of khaki satchel, and covered in inky scrawl and slogans. The sleeves of her jumper came down over hands, to her knuckles. Slithers of red varnish streaked her thumbnails, around the cuticle; it looked like blood where she'd bitten at the skin.

Juliet nudged me again and I tried not to look at her. She was holding her nose, and it was true, Sara did smell a bit. Not dirty exactly but sort of musty, like damp buildings.

At the end of tutorial, as we were getting ready to go

out, Juliet sniggered, 'Poor you,' just loud enough for Sara to hear.

Our school was an ancient 1960s comprehensive that had been randomly added to over the years, and now it sprawled across the tarmac and playing fields in a series of afterthoughts; pre-fab huts and slapped-up concrete blocks scattered all over, some connected by leaky-roofed corridors with plywood floors that bounced as you walked on them, and some not.

The Art block was right across the playground, well away from the main building. It was in what used to be the old dining hall. Sara followed me there, keeping back a little, like she didn't want to have to walk with me. Or she didn't want me to have to walk with her. I wasn't sure which. I had to keep looking round, to make sure she was still with me. She held her bag in front of her, clutched to her chest. It was a big, heavy-looking bag – God knows what she'd found to fill it with on her first day. Among all the other scrawl on it the words *John B is a wanker* stood out, underlined and ringed in thick black pen.

You could almost see the fence she'd got slapped up around her, almost read the keep out sign. But I did feel sorry for her. It must be awful being new, not knowing anyone, not having a clue where to go. And you don't need someone like Juliet making it worse.

I slowed right down, so she had to walk beside me. 'What school did you come from?' I asked, just for something to say.

'Kennington High,' she said, staring at the pavement in front of her. 'In Wanstead.'

Obviously I'd never heard of it. 'So have you just moved here, then?' I asked, but she didn't answer. She just kind of shrugged, which I thought was a bit odd. I mean, you've either moved or you haven't.

I tried a different tack. 'Do you like Art? We've just started a still life. Two empty bottles and a plant. Not exactly interesting but at least it won't go mouldy like the fruit we did last term. That was really gross.'

She smiled a little then, slightly. And she looked at me. 'At my old school you could bring your own things in for still life. Someone brought in a lobster once, a real one they'd got from the fish shop. They left it in the Art room over the Easter holidays.'

'Oh, yuk!' I laughed.

The smile widened a little more. 'It stank like you wouldn't believe when we went back,' she said.

When we got to the Art room I said, 'Look, don't take any notice of Juliet. She's OK really. You'll like her when you get to know her.'

She carried on looking at me but she didn't say anything. She didn't need to. The smile had gone and I knew what she was thinking. I could see it in her eyes.

* * *

Mrs Bevan sat Sara opposite me, with the still life between us. I studied her through the leaves of the geranium. For the whole hour she kept her eyes down, fixed on her drawing. It wasn't a very good drawing, all heavy dark lines, but then she hardly even glanced up at the still life in front of her. She seemed to have cocooned herself inside an invisible shell, shutting everything else out.

I thought she would feel me staring. At any minute I expected her to look up at me and say *What you staring at?* or something, but she didn't so I stared all the more. At fourteen she already had a cleft as deep as a knife slice between her eyebrows and thin lines at the sides of her mouth. It seemed incredible to me that anyone could hold on so tight to a frown.

Mrs Bevan always let us stay on through break if we wanted to, to finish off and tidy up. I love Art, and I'd always stay behind normally, but I wanted to see what Sara would do. I kind of felt responsible for her. Not because Mrs Rupert had asked me to look after her, but more because of what Juliet had said. I didn't want her to think we were all like Juliet.

As soon as the bell rang Sara picked up her bag to go, so I did the same and followed her out.

For a new person she seemed pretty intent on where she was going. She was already halfway down the path to the main playground by the time I caught up with her and stopped her.

'What are you going to do now?' I asked her. 'We always go in the quiet area at break. You can come with us if you like.'

I knew she'd say no. And to be honest I was glad. It was a bit like asking her to come and play with the tigers. I could just imagine Juliet's reaction if I waltzed over with Sara in tow.

'I don't think so,' she said, as if she could read my mind.

Her eyes were sort of flat, like an animal's. Opaque. She'd put lumpy mascara on the ends of her lashes but she'd missed the roots and I could see that they were the same colour as her hair, pale gingery-blonde. Strawberry-blonde, I think it's called. Yes I like that, strawberry-blonde.

'Not sure your friend would like that.'

I was going to lie and say *Oh yes, of course she would*, but then she said, 'And anyway, I'm meeting my brother.'

And off she went, gripping her bag against her body like a shield.

'Well I think she's common,' Juliet announced, biting into her apple. She shoved along the bench, trying to make more room for herself, bumping up against me with her bottom. She tossed her head and her hair flicked in my mouth, tasting of the revolting wax she used to hide her split ends, and annoying me. 'I mean, did you see those earrings? And she's got hard eyes.'

'Who's that boy she's with? Haven't seen him before, either,' Melanie said.

'Look at her flirting!' Juliet said, jabbing me with her elbow and spraying apple as she spoke. 'I knew she was just a tart.'

'That's her brother,' I said. You could tell that just by looking. They had the same colour hair and the same high, angular cheekbones. I watched them across the playground. They were both talking animatedly, and suddenly Sara laughed at something he said. The sound just reached me and I watched, fascinated as she smiled up at him.

'How do you know it's her brother?' Juliet demanded.

'She told me she was meeting him.'

Juliet snorted. 'Oh yeah? And what else did she tell you in your cosy tête-à-tête in the Art room?'

'Nothing.' I didn't tell them that I'd asked Sara to join us. Juliet would've loved that. *You did what?* she'd screech, outraged. *What would we want her hanging around us for?*

'Well I think he looks all right,' Melanie said and Juliet snorted again.

'If you like rough,' she bitched, but it was Sara I was watching. I couldn't believe how transformed she was now, talking to her brother, how her face just lit up and that angry, closed mask fell away.

Sara was standing at the gates when Juliet and I came out after school. I think she must have been waiting for her brother or something because she was looking back towards the school building and I saw her the minute we came out. She was standing with her weight leaning on one leg and her bag resting on her hip; when she saw us she stood up straight and pulled her bag up tight in front of her. I caught her eyes and smiled. For a second – and it could really only have been a second – it looked like she was going to smile back. But then even at that distance I saw the instant change as she brought the shutters *snap bang* down into place.

She stared into space as we walked past her, gaze fixed on some blank place just to the right of us. She was so defensive, so guarded up and I really felt for her. I really wanted to say something to her but it was difficult, you know, with Juliet right there. And Sara just kept staring into space. I could almost feel her, sussing us out, me along with Juliet, lumping us together.

And as we walked past her Juliet quipped, 'Ugh! What *is* that smell?' and it might as well have been me that said it, for all the damage it must have done.

* * *

I often called in at Juliet's on the way home from school but that week I had to go back with her every day, because it was her birthday on Saturday and she was having a party, and she wanted to talk about it and try on clothes. Juliet never got tired of trying on clothes. She'd been going on about this party since the end of last term; planning what to wear, who she was going to invite, what boy she wanted to get off with. She was inviting nine people from school: me, Hanna, Ruth and Melanie, and five boys. One for each of us. All her millions of cousins would be there too, along with the aunts and uncles, and family friends.

It was going to be a big family party, but then Juliet's family were big on everything. Juliet's dad was a builder and they had a huge house that he'd extended right across the back. There always seemed to be loads of people there, coming and going, talking in loud voices; there was always something going on.

It was just so different from my house. Sometimes I'd come back from Juliet's and the silence in our house would hit me. *Our* silence. It was more than just an absence. No one ever did anything unplanned in our house, no one ever just called round on the off-chance.

Juliet had two older brothers: one was in the Sixth-Form and the other was away at Uni most of the time. And her mum didn't work; she was always there when

9

we went back after school, doing the kind of things you always hoped your mother might do, baking cakes and things like that.

I'd always loved being at Juliet's house, and spent as much time as I could there. I suppose that's what happens when you're an only child. You latch on to other families, to make up for what you haven't got yourself. I mean, compared to Juliet's my family wasn't a family at all, just three little people, living their lives side by side.

It's funny how people's lives are. I used to look after Juliet's rabbit when she went on holiday, and twice a year our parents met and stood chatting while the bunny was stuck in the car. They were so different, our families. My parents looked small next to hers, dried up with thinking. Then on the way home I'd sit on the back seat with the rabbit in its hutch next to me, listening to my dad mutter, 'God, don't they go on,' and my mum reply, 'I thought we'd never get away.' Then they'd groan at the awfulness of Juliet's parents and have a quiet little laugh together about them. And I'd sit in the back, hating them for being so mean and so wrong.

By Friday I'd seen every possible outfit that Juliet could put together, but she still wanted me to go back with her for one last check, just to make sure. We let ourselves in the back door – Juliet didn't have a key, she didn't need one as her mum was always at home. In fact her mum had got in just before us, back from Sainsbury's. She'd picked up a bag of chocolate cookies for us while she was there.

'They're on the side there, girls,' she said, red-faced from bending down and unloading crisps and doughnuts and endless other goodies from plastic bags. You couldn't have so much as a biscuit in our house without getting a full-scale lecture on the dangers of eating between meals and messing with your glycaemic index. Juliet grabbed up the cookies, offered one to me, took one for herself, and another one, for the dog.

'Claudius!' she called. 'Claudius!'

We ate slowly, watching as her fat old Labrador waddled in from the living room and stopped at her feet, and half-stood, half-sat, salivating. He was disgusting, that dog. Juliet broke off a piece of cookie, waved it in front of his nose and then held it just too high up for him to reach, making him beg. He whined like he was in pain, and drooled all over the floor, and smacked his tail half-heartedly against the tiles. I thought this was gross, but Juliet loved the power. She said men were like dogs and she was just practising her skills.

Upstairs, I sat on Juliet's bed while she trawled through the contents of her wardrobe one more time. She had white fitted wardrobes with gold door knobs built around and over her bed, just like a mini version of the ones in her parents' room. Inside one of the doors was a full-length mirror; Juliet preened herself in front of it in one outfit after another. If she turned around and held up her little hand-mirror and looked into it she could get a look at her back view too. Tops, trousers, skirts were tried on and discarded and flung on to the bed, piling up around me.

It was all, *Did this make her look fat? Did this go with that? Would Oliver fancy her in this, did I think?* It washed over me in a soporific haze.

Clothes were not my thing at all but that didn't matter. You can't have two queen bees in a relationship. I was the plain one. I wasn't ugly or anything, but I wasn't blonde, I wasn't into clothes, I didn't worry about my figure all the time and I wasn't obsessed with boys. Juliet did enough of all that for both of us.

We'd been best friends since the Infants', Juliet and me. Since day one. It's just the way it had always been, always Juliet and Kate this, Juliet and Kate that. In fact we'd been friends so long I couldn't actually remember why we were friends any more.

When she'd finished trying on all her clothes, and finally fixed on an outfit, she started doing her nails. I lay back among the cushions and old teddies heaped up against the pink velvet headboard and watched her.

'So I'll wear the black skirt with my boots and the glittery top,' she said, painting Moonshine Silver on to her nails. 'And what about tights? Plain or patterned?' She didn't stop for my answer, which was just as well, as I doubt if I could have roused myself enough to reply anyway, but went on, 'And I'm going to straighten my hair.'

She waved her fingers about, drying them in the air. She'd got long, strong nails, Juliet. She was very proud of them. Every day she ate a cube of jelly, to keep those nails so nice. God knows what it did to her teeth – or her mind, for that matter, what with the bovine risk factor – but her nails were perfect, wide fat arcs on wide fat fingers. She always painted them, it was a little ritual every day when she got in from school. But then of course she'd have to take it all off again in the morning because we weren't allowed to wear nail varnish in school. The bin under her dressing table was heaped full of cotton wool puffs, stained with every colour imaginable and squashed flat where she'd pressed them against her nails.

When the nails were dry she got out a little sheet of foil stars, and started peeling them off, and pressing them on to the tips. 'What are you going to wear?' she asked, but I could tell she wasn't interested.

'Oh I don't know,' I said. 'My jeans, probably.'

I watched as she pressed the last stars into place, then held her hands up, fingers extended, and admired the results. Suddenly she looked at me, and said. 'Come with me. I've got something to show you.'

Slowly I uncurled myself from the cosiness of her bed, and followed her out of the room. On the landing she gestured for me to stay quiet, and listened to make sure no one was about to come upstairs, then she crept along to her brother's room, the oldest brother, the one who'd left home. She sneaked inside and I followed her, careful not to creak the door as I closed it behind us. It was a very plain, boring, boy's room, with nothing much in it now that he'd moved out except the bed and the furniture and a few old books. Juliet went straight for the bed and pulled out a pile of magazines from underneath it.

'Shit!' she hissed, looking at her hand and shaking it. 'I've smudged my nail!'

I lifted up the top magazine, curious, but she grabbed it off me.

'Look at this,' she said. 'You're not going to believe this.' She turned the pages quickly, shoving image after image into my face. I thought it would be just a load of topless women but it wasn't, it was real bad stuff, *horrible* stuff, close-up photos taken from all angles of open mouths and open legs and men with big dicks sticking it, ramming it in.

Gross, really gross.

Juliet turned the pages, hand over her mouth, giggling. I looked at those pictures and I looked up at her face, bright-eyed and bloated behind her hand, and I giggled too.

But I thought it was disgusting. It is, isn't it? It's disgusting.

I gave Juliet a pair of earrings for her birthday. Little silver half-moons that sat right on the lobe.

'Thanks,' she said, but she didn't put them on. She was wearing some big gold dangly ones that her brother had given her. That same brother that kept the dirty magazines under his bed. I looked at him, with his little round glasses and his short, gelled-back hair and tried to imagine him looking at those pictures. I couldn't.

They had a big living room that opened up into the dining room; everyone was in there at first, eating, talking, making a lot of noise. But Juliet's mum had cleared out the playroom for us and the cousins, and we escaped out there as soon as we could. Juliet had got a new CD player for her birthday, and she brought it in and turned all the lights off except for one little lamp. Straight away she put on a slow CD and started flirting like mad with Oliver Bennett, her choice for the night, while the rest of us sat around and watched. She grabbed hold of his hand, pulling him to his feet, and made him dance with her. She draped herself all over him, pressing her body right up against his, and shoving her hair into his face. He didn't seem to object.

'Come on,' she said over his shoulder to the rest of us. 'Don't just sit there. *Dance*. It is my birthday.'

It seemed Juliet always got what she wanted, especially on her birthday. The rest of us paired up as required, and shuffled round the room. I danced with Ed Stevens, robot-like, while he rubbed his hands up and down my back so fast I thought he might start a fire.

Still, we were pretty safe. Not much could happen with the whole of Juliet's extended family in the next room.

Of course, after the party Juliet wanted to talk about it even more.

She'd whisper to me in tutorial, with her hand up by her mouth, half hiding her face, making it clear that her words were for select ears only. She'd whisper really quietly so that I'd have to put my head right up close to hers, and so collude in the secrecy. She had nothing much to say, just wasn't Oliver gorgeous and did I think he'd fancied her in that top? But that wasn't the point. It didn't matter what she was saying. What mattered was that she and I had secrets, and that Sara mustn't hear.

It was pretty pathetic really. It was obvious to me that Sara couldn't care less about Juliet's stupid party.

We were walking down the corridor on our way to Maths, and it just so happened that Sara was a little way ahead of us, on her own. Seeing her, Juliet grabbed my arm and speeded us both up so that we were walking right behind her. Then she snorted loudly, like she was trying not to laugh. Sara's shoulders tensed, almost imperceptibly, and she carried on walking, ignoring us.

Beside me Juliet was gesticulating frantically, trying to think up something bitchy to say. I could feel my heart shrinking back inside me and I stopped walking. Juliet yanked on my arm, trying to pull me on.

'Oh,' she said loudly, quickly, before Sara was out of earshot. 'I hadn't realized that the tramp look was back in this season, had you, Kate?'

Irritation flashed up through my body. She'd used my name, lumping me together with her. It's what she always did. She just assumed that because she thought it was amusing to bitch about Sara I would too.

Sara sat at the front in English, right at the front next to Eleanor Rees, because that was the only space there was. We'd been in the same class for English since Year Eight and we sat next to the same person, in twos, the desks all arranged in rows, facing the front. A girl with greasy yellow hair that nobody had taken a great deal of notice of used to sit at the front, next to Eleanor, but she'd left the school halfway through Year Nine and nobody had moved around and filled her space, so Eleanor had remained on her own, till now.

There was a definite hierachy in English; Sara came

in right at the bottom. The boys sat on one side of the class, the girls on the other. Juliet and I sat right at the back, next to the window, with Ruth and Hanna next to us, and Jane and Melanie next to them. Then came all the other girls, and Sara sat right at the front, next to Eleanor Rees.

We used to pass little notes along the back between the six of us; Juliet would start it, writing some witty little remark on a tiny piece of paper folded even tinier, then we'd pass it along between us when the teacher wasn't looking, each of us unfolding it, reading it, folding it back up again and passing it on. When Melanie got it she'd add some little comment of her own before folding the note back up and sending it back, then we'd each do the same, unfolding it again and adding our own little bit in tiny, tiny writing then folding it back up again and passing it back towards Juliet. These comments were always a bit on the bitchy side. It was easy to sit at the back and be superior, to notice that Megan was too fat to do her zip up properly and that you could see her knickers through the gap, or that Nicola's dandruff was getting worse. But now these notes were always about Sara. *You-know-who's looking a bit rough this morning, wouldn't you say?* Juliet wrote, starting it off, and I passed it along. When the note came back to me they'd all added *No rougher than usual, iron must be on the blink again,* and *What iron?* Nothing too bad to start with, and it was easy enough for me to write *The iron she forgot to use*. That's what I did at first, I just wrote some little nothing comment like *The poor girl can't help it* or *Now, now, girls, don't pick on the afflicted*. But the notes got bitchier and bitchier. It became *Where's the rotten fish? It's in SW's knickers*, and things like that. Really nasty. I stopped passing them along and Juliet hated that. She still wrote her notes, but she'd pointedly lean past me and pass them straight to Ruth, and on the way back Ruth would do the same, stretching out across the aisle when Mrs Harris wasn't looking, by-passing me. I suspect, after a while, the notes stopped being about Sara and started being about me.

All relationships have a final cut-off point. They have to have, or they'd go on fizzling out forever. Maybe Juliet and I would have carried on fizzling out forever if Sara hadn't come along. I don't know. But there has to be a final thing, a final betrayal, a *last straw* – and I did it, that last straw. I chose Sara in netball, instead of Juliet.

I was good at netball, so more often than not I was Centre, and Centre picked the team. This time, I was picking one team, and Melanie was picking the other, and I had to choose first. I knew Melanie wouldn't pick Sara. I knew that if I did what I ought to do, what everyone *thought* I would do, I would pick Juliet first as I always did and Sara would be left till last, till after the too-slow girl and the too-tall girl and the too-fat girl – till the very last; left staring at the ground, unwanted.

I don't know what made me do it; I picked Sara straight away.

She looked up when I called out her name and I swear it was like the clouds moved out of her face. And when she came and stood next to me it felt right. It felt so, so right.

I didn't look at Juliet, I didn't dare; but I could feel her glaring at me. I could feel Melanie glaring at me; *everyone* was glaring at me but I didn't care. I felt like shouting, like jumping up and down and running round and round the playground. I'd really blown it this time. I'd blown it but I'd done it.

I'd chosen Sara.

2

Hot September closed with days of endless, relentless rain. It fell straight down from the sky as if the ground was a magnet, and hit the pavement outside with such force that it bounced up again. From where I sat I could watch the rain and Sara. She was sitting two rows in front of me. I could see the points of her spine through her jumper as she slouched over her desk and the curve of her left ear. While I watched she pushed her hair back behind it, and I saw the backs of her earrings and the redness of the skin around them.

'Kate! You won't pass your Biology GCSE by staring out of the window. Now pay attention, please.' Mrs Lewis rapped on her table with her ruler. 'Now, today we are going to do something different. An experiment in mind over matter.' There were a couple of giggles. 'An exploration of the senses.' More giggles and Mrs Lewis beamed like an actor before an audience. 'The sense of taste, to be precise. I want you to get in pairs. But not your usual pairs; this time I want you to pair up with someone new, someone you don't know very well . . .'

Chairs were scraped back and noise broke out. 'No, Emma, Helen, this is not an excuse for a pre-lunch gossip,' Mrs Lewis called out. 'Sophie! Put Paul down. Keep your love life till after school, *please*.'

Sara made no effort to pair up with anyone. She stayed exactly where she was, hunched over her desk, as if she didn't even expect to be included. Before anyone else could latch on to me I squeezed between the tables to reach her. She lifted her head then, and I wondered if she'd even heard what Mrs Lewis had been saying; she looked half asleep, miles away.

'I'll go with you,' I said, and for a second she looked like she wondered what I was talking about. Then the fog in her eyes lifted slightly.

'Oh,' she said. 'Right.'

And I wondered what she could've been thinking about, that could block her right out like that.

It was an experiment about taste; about how different tastes are more easily identified on different areas of the tongue. We had four droppers containing the four major tastes: saline, sweet, bitter and sour, and had to take it in turns to guess which was which, and say on which part of the tongue they tasted strongest. I tested Sara first. She sat facing me with her eyes closed and I noticed how pale the skin on her face was, especially around her eyes where little blue veins trickled out across her eyelids. A nerve flickered on her left eyelid but other than that she was perfectly still. I dropped the solutions on to her tongue in turn but it was Sara I was studying. Her front teeth had grooves down them and were quite yellow, and when she closed her mouth to taste the solution her throat moved up and down as she swallowed.

All around us people were shrieking with laughter and Mrs Lewis kept shouting, 'Calm down, class, calm down,' but Sara and I were silent except for when she spoke to name the tastes. My heart was beating heavily, slowly. I moved my hand carefully, so as not to spill the solution. I could even see the tiny white downy hairs on her cheeks.

Then it was Sara's turn to test me and she did it so much quicker, knocking her knees against mine as she leant forward. Her breath sighed across my face in nicotine-scented puffs.

The bell went for lunch. I opened my eyes and Sara was already stuffing her books into her bag.

'Right, I want you to write up your findings for homework,' Mrs Lewis was shouting over the noise, '*Homework!*'

'See you later,' Sara said, then she was gone, out the door. I gathered my things up as fast as I could, and followed her out.

She was halfway down the corridor already, ahead of everybody else. 'Sara, wait!' I called, and I squashed my way through the others, running to catch her up. She was walking like she couldn't wait to get out of there.

'What are you doing now?' I asked, and I could feel my heart beating fast, from chasing after her. 'Where are you going?'

'Home,' she said. She slowed down a little and relaxed her grip on her bag, sliding it round so it was perched on one hip, away from me. She'd been growing out her fringe, for ages by the look of it. It fell down in her face and she blew upwards fluttering it out of her eyes as she looked at me. 'I only live round the corner,' she said. 'You can come with me if you like.'

For just a split second I thought of Juliet and the others sitting on our bench, waiting for me. And of all those chilly shoulders that had been mine to endure since the netball incident. I barely hesitated but it was still enough to dim the warmth back out of Sara's face.

'Don't let me force you,' she said stiffly, and she hoiked her bag back up into place, clamping it against her chest. And she started walking fast again, like that was it: conversation over.

'You won't,' I said, trying to be flippant. 'Really.' I had to practically run, just to keep up with her. 'I just thought you'd never ask.' I wanted to make her laugh. She didn't, but she smiled the faintest of smiles, glancing sideways at me through her hair. I wondered what it was that I could see in her eyes: acceptance, promise? I don't know. But I smiled back, trying not to think about all the things that Juliet would say about me, now.

I had the weirdest feeling, like walking along a cliff edge in the dark.

Sara's house was a sort of chalet-style bungalow with rooms built into the roof. The pebbledash was cracked and paint was peeling off the window frames, showing old people's blue under the white. She must have seen something on my face because she said, 'It's not ours, we're just renting it for a while till the divorce comes through. We got this because my mum's sister lives up the road.'

We went in the back door because she said the front door stuck. It opened into the kitchen, which was tiny, and even though we'd both been huddling under my umbrella we were still soaked and walked wet muddy footprints all over the orange lino. I closed my umbrella and the water ran off it; I went to put it in the sink but there were dishes and old teabags there, so I propped it against the tap instead. We'd steamed up the window, so it seemed dark outside. Little drops of rain were seeping in through a hole in the frame and running along the ridges in the wood, loosening up the mould.

'Sit down,' Sara said, and cleared a pile of newspapers off the table and dumped them on the floor instead. I pulled out a chair; it had a black plastic back and was sticky. When I sat down I tried to wipe my fingers on my skirt but the material stuck to them.

There were no fitted units in the kitchen, just old-fashioned cupboards around the sink, a fridge, and a cooker that stood on its own. They had one of those funny old-fashioned kettles sitting on top of the cooker, you know, one of those ancient metal things that you heat up like a saucepan to boil. Sara lifted the kettle, shook it to see if it was empty then turned on the tap to fill it. Nothing happened at first and she muttered, 'Come on . . .' Then when the water did come out, a great clanking noise echoed round the pipes. Then she rummaged in her bag for matches, and went through at least five trying to light a gas ring for the kettle and the grill. Each time she let the match burn right up to her fingers and yelped, 'Shit!' before flinging it into the sink.

I wondered why she didn't just use the toaster and the proper kettle, plugged in next to the fridge. And then I saw the socket that they were plugged into. It was hanging away from the wall. Someone had undone the top two screws holding it in place and disconnected the wires. One of the wires was sticking out, with sticky tape wrapped around the end, and the plastic underneath the kettle plug had melted out of shape and gone a dark orange colour.

'Do you want toast?' Sara asked as she slapped sliced white bread under the grill.

'No thanks. I've got my sandwiches,' I said, feeling like such a mummy's girl suddenly with my packed lunch. I watched as Sara stuck a cigarette in her mouth and dipped down with her head sideways to light it at the gas under the kettle. She held her hair back from her face and her cheeks puffed in and out. Then she took one long drag, laid the cigarette on the draining board, opened the fridge, sniffed the milk and slopped it into two mugs. She took teabags from a packet in the cupboard next to the sink, said, 'Sugar?' and plonked the packet on the table. By then the toast needed turning and the kettle was just beginning to hiss. She pulled the grill pan out, flipped the toast, poured water on to the tea, opened the fridge again for butter, and just caught the toast from burning. Her cigarette had gone out. 'Fuck,' she said, and had to relight it with a match this time because she'd turned the gas out. I sat and watched all this, feeling that if I so much as moved I'd break her concentration.

Sara put the mugs and plate of toast on the table. The black plastic surface was covered in a million ghostly rings from all the teacups that had scalded it since God knows when. Sara sat down, balanced what was left of her cigarette on the side of her plate, and started to eat.

27

'Is that all you're having?' I asked.

'Mmm,' she said through a mouthful of toast. 'Go on then. Eat your sandwiches.'

But suddenly I didn't feel like eating the cheese and salad rolls that my mum had foil-wrapped for me that morning. 'I'm not hungry,' I said. 'I'll have them later.'

She shrugged. *Please yourself.* She bent her head down over her plate as she ate, and a strand of hair caught in the butter and stuck to the toast. She peeled the hair away and flicked it back over her shoulder and it dangled down her back, butter still glued to the end. I felt dead awkward, just sitting there, watching her eat. I desperately tried to think of something to say. I'd come this far and now I was floundering: and I couldn't bear that she'd think I was a geek, or a snob, or anything like that.

I wanted her to like me.

'Does your brother come home for lunch?' I knew it was a stupid question, but I couldn't think of anything else to say.

Again she shrugged. 'Sometimes.'

'He looks nice, your brother. You look really close.'

'We are,' she said, like it was a full stop.

I sipped at my tea. It was so strong that it stung the top of my mouth. 'I wish I had a brother,' I said. 'Or a sister.' And then I thought what a pathetic thing that was to say, and what on earth did I expect her to say back? She said nothing, just carried on eating her toast without looking at me. I was losing her. She'd never invite me again. The clock above the door said 12.55. We only had about ten minutes or so until we had to get back.

'Is your mum at work?' Another stupid question. I pinched at the skin on my hand, hating myself. Sara stuck the last bit of toast in her mouth, picked up the cigarette which had nearly gone out and puffed on it a couple of times to get it going again as she chewed.

'She's got her own shop.' She looked at me then, as if I'd be surprised, as if I wouldn't believe her. 'A fabric shop, in North Shere. Well, it's both of theirs really – Mum and Dad's – but since they split he's left it all to her, all the bills and everything. He's a bastard and I hate him.' She stubbed her cigarette out on the plate, then leant over to get another one out of her bag.

'Can I have one?' It was out before I thought. She stopped and looked at me.

'I bet you've never smoked a cigarette in your life.'

'No,' I said, 'but I want one now.'

She was looking at me as if she thought I was mad. I held her gaze. I didn't want her to think I was mad, I wanted her to think I was like her. Or at least that I *could* be like her.

I thought for a second she was going to say no. I thought she was going to go all moral on me and tell me she didn't want to be responsible for starting me smoking, or something like that. But then she shrugged. 'All right, then,' she said, and offered me the packet.

I took a cigarette, and stuck it between my lips.

'Well don't bum it,' she said. 'It's not a dummy.' She took one for herself and put it in her mouth. 'Like this,' she said, and the cigarette bobbed as she spoke. 'You just hold it between your lips. You don't suck on it.'

She struck a match and held it for me, and burnt her fingers on it as I puffed and sucked and tried to get a light. 'Jesus,' she said, striking up another. 'What are you doing?'

Again I puffed and sucked, and again the match burnt down to Sara's fingers. 'Stop sucking,' she said, really slowly, like she was talking to an idiot. 'Just draw in gently.' She ripped a third match along the side of the box and raised the flame to me. 'This is the last time,' she said. 'That cigarette is so slimed up it's making me want to heave. And I'm not wasting another.'

The match fizzled down to her fingers and went out.

I stared at her over the length of the cigarette poking out from my mouth, and she stared back. Suddenly, she started to laugh. She looked like she did that time in the playground, on her first day, laughing at something her brother had said. It was like a piece of sunshine had slipped down inside her and lent her an escape.

I laughed too, and the cigarette got even wetter. I

can't tell you how gross it was, keeping it stuck in my mouth. Slime isn't the word for it. And it tasted foul, like the bottom of ashtrays. And it wasn't even lit.

'Give it here,' Sara said, when she stopped laughing. She took it from my mouth and wiped it on her sleeve, grimacing. Then she stuck it in her mouth, alongside her own, and lit them both with the same match. Mine took a little longer to get going than hers, but she did it, and then she handed it to me, pulling a face like she wanted to gag. 'That is just so bummed,' she said. 'You'll have to do better than that.'

I took the cigarette back and put it in my mouth. It was wet from me, wet from her; it felt like a kiss. I felt this sudden charge going through me, and breathed in, quick. My mouth filled with smoke; I didn't know what to do with it. It hit the back of my throat and made me gag. I couldn't breathe, I couldn't swallow. I coughed and coughed like there was acid spilling down my throat, while Sara whacked me on the back, and half-killed herself, laughing.

We had PE after lunch. Sara's house was just a couple of minutes from the school but even so we were nearly late. We ran into the changing room still laughing at my attempt at smoking, but then the laughter stopped dead. Everyone else was already in there, getting changed, and they all stopped talking when we came in. Then Juliet said, really loudly so that everyone could hear, 'Oh it's Kate with her new best friend. Been slumming it?'

'For God's sake, Juliet—' I hissed.

'Traitor!' Her eyes filled with tears, and Melanie and Hanna gathered around her and she turned away. I looked at Sara. She was hanging her bag on her peg but I could see her face, set hard again, mask back in place.

'Oh come on, Juliet.' I put out my hand to try to turn her round to look at me but Melanie and Hanna clamped themselves together in my way, like a closed barrier, blocking me out.

'Leave it,' Hanna said. 'You've done enough. You've been with her – you *smell* like her.'

'Oh for God's sake!' I stuck my bag on the hook next to Sara's. She was already getting undressed. Her knickers were tatty and grey as if something dark had been washed with the whites by mistake. The tops of her legs were sort of mottled. I could imagine how they would look when she was old. She put on her PE skirt but she kept on the top that she'd been wearing under her jumper. I noticed this, and so did everyone else. How could she stand it? How could she bear to hear the things they were saying? I wanted to feel angry for her but instead I just felt sad.

I couldn't believe I'd been friends with such bitches for so long.

Well not any more.

I started going around with Sara all the time after that, and every lunchtime we went back to her house. Sometimes Glenn, her brother, came back too, and sometimes he'd bring his friends with him. Then we'd all crowd around that little table in the kitchen, drinking endless cups of tea and smoking, if anyone had any fags.

I guess it felt pretty good, hanging out with guys from Year Eleven.

But it felt even better when it was just Sara and me.

3

'Not seen much of Juliet lately, love,' my dad said, shovelling spaghetti into his mouth. He always wrapped too much round his fork, working on the theory that half of it would fall off again midway between plate and mouth. Often it didn't, though. Often he'd just end up having to stuff too much in, with errant strands flipping about, splashing bolognaise sauce all over his chin. 'You two fallen out?'

I twirled a tiny amount of spaghetti round my fork and just pulled a face at Dad. Ten out of ten for noticing the obvious, I thought. He'd got a big red dollop of sauce just beside his mouth, which was really quite revolting. I hate spaghetti; it's just too annoying to eat. And I hated having to watch my dad tucking in with such gusto, like he fancied himself as an Italian peasant or something. What is it with parents when they're eating foreign food? Like when they're on holiday, enthusing over the paella in Spain or braving the snails in France. It's like they think they can eat their way out of suburbia.

'Oh Juliet's old news,' Mum said. 'It's Sara now.' *She* ate her spaghetti the posh way, using the side of her fork to cut it up into small pieces before pushing it on to her spoon.

'Sara? Not heard that name before.'

'She's new,' I said. I wondered what Sara would be having for supper – only in her house they called it tea and ate it on their laps in front of the TV.

'Ah,' Dad grunted through a mouthful, still piling it all in. 'Pass the parmesan, Gina, love.'

'Oh yes, it's Sara this, Sara that,' Mum said, smiling at me. 'You're out of touch, Tony.' Then she carefully passed the plate with the little block of cheese on it, and the parmesan grater. Not for us the pre-grated stuff in your handy little tub. We had to have the real stuff, shipped all the way over from Parma to the deli in Lewiston, and cut off the block.

'Ah.' Dad took the parmesan and the grater then paused for a moment, head to one side slightly, as if considering this new information. Then he said, 'So, Juliet is no more.'

'Well, you know how it is at that comp, Tony.'

Always *that comp*. And Mum never missed a chance to say it. Whenever there was any mention of school, anything at all even remotely to do with school, Mum would look to heaven in that way and say *I don't know what you get up to at that comp* or *Goodness knows what goes on at that comp* or *Heaven only knows what that comp is thinking of.* They were going to send me to the girls' school in South Shere and pay for me to wear a blue-and-gold uniform complete with blazer and tie, but my dad loves to tell me how he believes that education ought to be the right of everyone and not just the privilege of the few, and at the last minute he'd put his foot down and they'd sent me to the comp.

We have a duty to support our local school, he'd say, like he was doing the world a favour. I wonder if he's still saying that now.

My dad likes to think himself a very *honourable* man, a very *principled* man, but his principles let him down the first time he dropped me off at Sara's house one Saturday afternoon. It was raining or I'd have walked. As he pulled up he peered across me out the window and said, 'Bit shabby, isn't it, love?'

'Well that's hardly her fault,' I turned on him, outraged.

'Whoah!' he said, raising his hands, palms up, a gesture half-defensive, half-calming. 'I never said it was!'

'It's her dad's fault.' I snapped, condemning him along with all dads. 'He left them and their old house has been sold and all the money's gone on debts and Sara's mum has to work all the time trying to keep their business going but there's no money and it's all her dad's fault!' I finished because I was out of breath and suddenly my chest felt so tight that I knew I'd start crying if I said anything else.

'Calm down, Kate,' my dad said in that half-laughing, half-embarrassed way, looking at me all taken aback, like I'd just thrown the most amazing outsize tantrum.

I didn't calm down, but I did shut up. That's what we all do in our family. No one ever talks about anything big.

Inside, the kitchen stank of gas.

'It's this stupid heater,' Sara explained. 'It's useless. But the boiler's packed up again and this is all we've got. Glenn's gone to borrow another one from Aunty Sheila.'

It was boiling in the kitchen but Sara said the rest of the house was freezing. 'It's all right in here,' she said. 'This thing was working all right earlier.' She kicked the gas heater, which was hissing out gas but not heating it. 'It's like a witch's arse in my bedroom.'

The back door opened and Glenn came in, wet from the rain. He said, 'All right, Kate?' to me, and to Sara, 'Rachel's just coming,' and went to fill the kettle and light the cooker, filling the room with more gas. I watched the match nervously, but at least he'd left the back door open. Rain pattered down from the top of the door frame on to the floor inside.

Sara said, 'For Christ's sake, Glenn,' and would have

closed the door but then there was the sound of footsteps running up the path, and a girl appeared in the doorway, with a little electric heater tucked under one arm, the cord wrapped round her wrist like a tail. Raindrops clung to the ends of her brown curly hair and she shook her head like a dog. Her face was as open as Sara's was closed.

'Hiya, Sara. Got this for you.'

'Cheers,' Sara said, taking the heater as Rachel stamped her wet feet in the doorway, in the space where a doormat should have been. 'It's bloody freezing in here. I'm going to stick this in the hall. I'll put it on full blast. It's got the whole house to warm up.' Then, like it was an afterthought, she stopped and did the introductions. 'Oh, Kate this is Rachel,' she said, 'my cousin. And Rachel this is Kate, my best friend.' She opened the door from the kitchen into the rest of the house and cold air blasted in. I couldn't see that one electric heater was going to make much difference, but still Sara went out into the hall, looking for somewhere to plug it in.

I sat at the kitchen table, basking in the fact that she'd called me her best friend.

Rachel sat down opposite me. 'Not for me,' she said, as Glenn began putting mugs out for tea. 'I can't stay long. I just wanted to check we're all still on for tonight.'

'Yeah, still on,' Glenn said. 'You coming round tonight, Kate?'

'No, I—'

'Yeah, why don't you stay, Kate?' Sara said as she came back into the kitchen. 'It'll be a laugh. Glenn's got his mates coming round too.' She pulled a big-eyed face for emphasis and said, '*Andy* and *Mark*.'

'D'you know Andy and Mark, Kate?' Rachel asked.

'Well, a bit—'

'Course she does,' Sara interrupted. Then she said, 'Rachel's *in love* with Mark—'

'And Sara's *in love* with Andy,' Rachel teased back.

'Oh great,' Glenn said, tossing teabags into the mugs. 'And what am I supposed to do while you two get off with my mates?'

Sara and Rachel looked at each other, then both spoke at once. 'Watch the football!'

'I wish I could stay,' I said, as I followed Sara up the wooden stairs into the roof. Rachel had gone home and Glenn was watching TV in the front room. It was a quarter to five and already getting dark; I would really have to be going soon.

'Well stay then,' Sara said, like it was that simple. There were only two rooms upstairs and the landing was too small for both of us. She nodded her head to the right, said, 'That's Glenn's,' then went into the other room.

'I can't,' I said as I followed her in. 'Not just like that. My mum and dad would never let me.'

'Well next week, then. Ask them. Stay the night. Go on, it'll be a laugh.'

I had never been in Sara's room before. I looked around and thought of my own bedroom with its matching pine furniture and Laura Ashley prints and the pale yellow that Mum and I chose for the carpet and walls when we had it redecorated last year. Sara's room didn't have a carpet. There was a stripy woven rug on the floorboards between two beds which both sagged under the assorted quilts and blankets that covered them. There was no wardrobe. Her clothes were piled on a chair. I thought they were dirty clothes, waiting to be washed but she said, 'Jesus, it's freezing in here,' ferreted through for a jumper, shook it out and pulled it on. Then she went over to the dressing table by the window, where the roof sloped down, took a packet of cigarettes from the clutter on top, said, 'Here,' and gave me one. She lit her own with a match, puffed on it for a bit, then handed it to me for me to light my own from the burning nib of hers, like she'd shown me. Sara pulled the sleeves of her jumper down over her hands, forced open the sash window, and we leant out, puffing foggy smoke into the damp air.

'Rachel's nice,' I said.

'Yeah she is, she's great. Her mum's really nice too and helped us get this place, you know, when we had nowhere else to go. But her stepdad, Ron, is a total bastard. He won't let Rachel out at all except to come round here; she's nearly sixteen but she's not allowed to even talk to boys, which is why she goes to St Mary's.'

'Really? I nearly ended up there,' I said, and immediately wished I hadn't.

Sara gave me a funny look. 'Oh yeah?' she said. 'Poor you. Well anyway, Rachel's been seeing Glenn's mate Mark for about a month now, but they can only meet here. You should come tonight,' she said again. 'It'll be a real laugh. I'm seeing Andy.'

I wasn't exactly sure what Sara meant when she said she was 'seeing' Andy. I hadn't even known that she particularly liked him, until now. He'd been back to the house a few times at lunch with Glenn, and sure, she did sit on his knee sometimes. But it was like that when there were a few of us; you sat wherever you could.

'Here,' Sara said suddenly and stubbed her cigarette out on the windowsill. 'I've got something for you.'

She began to rummage through the tubes and bottles of make-up scattered over the dressing table. 'Come here,' she said. 'I got this the other day. I got it for you. I thought it would suit you.'

It was a lipstick, one of those testers they have at the chemist's, with a little plastic lipstick showing the colour on the lid. She took the top off and twisted it up: bright pink and hardly used. With one hand she held the top of my arm to steady herself, and with the other she dragged the colour slowly and thickly across my mouth. Her elbow jabbed into my chest. I stood still, watching her eyes as they watched my lips.

'There.' She turned back to the dressing table and rummaged. 'This is my favourite.' She coloured her own lips with an old stub of red.

Then she stepped back a fraction and we both looked into the mirror. 'Suits you,' she said. 'You should wear make-up more often.'

My clown's face peered with her, trying to smile.

I thought about her all evening and wondered what she was doing. I could imagine them in that house, drinking beer or cider, and smoking and sitting on the brown draylon sofa and chairs in that freezing cold living room, with the fumes from that terrifying gas heater intoxicating the air. I envied them their closeness. I wondered who would be sitting where. Maybe the TV was on and the boys were watching the football or something. They didn't have a DVD. They only had an old video recorder that didn't record things any more and was pretty useless at playing them too, Sara said. They didn't have a CD player either because Sara's dad had got it, though they could have brought the radio-cassette player in from the kitchen. Perhaps Rachel was sitting next to Mark, or on his lap even. I hardly knew Mark; I couldn't imagine him speaking or think what he might say to Rachel, how he would tell her that he loved her. *If* he loved her. There was only room for three on the sofa. Perhaps Sara sat there too, next to Rachel and Mark. Or on one of the chairs; Glenn would be in the other chair. I couldn't place Andy at all; certainly not with Sara, sitting with her, being with her, doing whatever 'seeing' her meant.

My dad always did the cooking in our house on Saturday nights, getting something out of a recipe book and making a great mess in the kitchen. He fancied himself quite the chef. I even remember what it was that night: grilled sardines with some funny couscous stuff; the kitchen stank for days. I ate the sardines and helped Mum clear up and half-watched some film on DVD, but all the time it was going round and round in my head: *Sara, Sara, Sara.* I was in bed at eleven. I lay in the dark, still wondering what she was doing. I thought of her bed and how cold it would be when she got into it. The lipstick she gave me was in the top drawer of my dressing table; I had no other make-up. I thought of her face and her whiter-than-white skin and of the too-pink foundation that she smeared all over it like a mask, stopping at her jaw and leaving just her neck pure and clean.

In the morning when I went down to breakfast my dad was already there with the papers and coffee. I made myself some toast and spread one slice with honey and the other with black-cherry jam, and I wondered if Sara was up yet and thought of her padding down to that little kitchen to battle with the gas and the kettle and sliced white from a packet. The bathroom was next to the kitchen in their house, with a loo that was hard to flush in a tiny room next to that. It was only October but cold already with a bitter wind that would hiss like a bitch through the cracks in sash windows; too cold for a bath at Sara's house.

'Dad, can I stay at Sara's next Saturday?'

'Mmm?'

'Can I stay at Sara's?'

He didn't even look up from his newspaper. 'I suppose so. If it's OK with her mum.'

I'd never met Sara's mum. She was always at the shop or round Aunty Sheila's or, according to Sara, consoling herself with a bottle somewhere. I could only picture Sara in that kitchen, lighting the grill to make toast, pouring tea for her and Glenn. I couldn't wait to see her on Monday, to tell her I could come.

4

On Saturday morning I walked round the corner to the chemist's and bought a black kohl pencil from the Rimmel stand, so I could do my eyes the way Sara did hers. I spent the afternoon in my room, practising. I'd read in some magazine that if you drew it on in little feathery strokes it looked more natural, but when I tried this it just looked all jagged, so I had to rub it off with tissue and start again. I hadn't thought to buy any eye make-up remover. I hadn't thought to buy a special eyeliner sharpener either but the chemist near us shut at lunchtime on Saturdays so I had to make do with the sharpener from my pencil case. The hole in the sharpener was too big and the kohl was soft and kept breaking against the blade; I ended up wasting half the eyeliner before I'd hardly begun.

I often watched Sara put her eyeliner on. She wore it every day to school even though we weren't supposed to. By lunchtime it had always worn off and she'd have to do it again. She'd pull the skin under her eye down and draw right along the rim, in little strokes, right into the corner. Then she'd do the upper lid, tilting her head up as far as she could, which meant she had to strain her

eyes to see what she was doing in the mirror. She'd pull
her eyelashes back with the fingers on her other hand
and draw along the upper rim, starting at the inner
corner and working along, into the roots of her lashes.

I tried to do it the way Sara did but I hated pulling
the skin away from my eyes and seeing all that red down
inside the socket. And when I drew kohl inside the rims
it made my eyes smart, and the kohl smudged, dirtying
up the whites so I had to blink a lot and wait for my eyes
to clear before trying again. In the end I drew around
the outside of the rims, trying to keep the line as close
to my lashes as I could. It was hard to stop it going on
too thick, and it was hard to make both eyes match. But
I did OK. I thought that if it looked just a tiny bit . . .
well . . . *heavy* it was just because it was different and I
wasn't used to seeing myself like that. Sara's eyes were
wide but mine are small and round. And dark. The
eyeliner made them look darker, like black buttons
peeping out from under my fringe.

I decided to wear my jeans because I thought Sara
would be wearing hers, and my black V-neck top with
the little buttons down the front. And my brown chunky
cardi; I knew I'd be cold at Sara's. I spent half the
afternoon getting ready and the rest of it looking at
myself in the mirror, adopting different poses, having
imaginary conversations in my head and trying out every
expression I could think of. I'd never looked at myself in

this way before, never tried to see myself as somebody else would. As Sara would.

'Eyeliner?' my dad said, as if he'd never seen the stuff before. 'Bit much, isn't it, Kate?'

'No.' Instantly I felt on guard, defensive. It probably was a bit much the way I'd done it but no way was I taking it off again. I tried to keep my face turned away from him so he couldn't stare at me like that.

He hovered in my bedroom doorway, getting in my way as I pushed past him to get my toothbrush from the bathroom. I wished he'd go away and leave it at that but I knew he wouldn't. He was still there when I came back from the bathroom, waiting for me. Hovering with intent. I avoided his eye but I could feel him staring at me. I could almost feel him thinking.

'Who's going to be there tonight?' he asked as I squeezed back round him again, stuffing my things into my bag.

'No one. Just me and Sara,' I lied, keeping busy with my bag.

'So where will you sleep?' he went on – and honestly, what kind of a question is that? Where did he think I was going to sleep?

'In Sara's room,' I said, and I'd have looked him square in the eye then except I didn't want him to start on about the make-up again. 'She's got a spare bed.

And her mum will sleep in her room and her brother in his. OK?'

I thought he was going to tell me he wanted to come and check out Sara's room for himself, or something stupid, but he just looked at me hard and said, 'I'll ring you later, then. To make sure you're all right.'

I zipped up my bag and stared back at him in exasperation. 'I'm not a baby, Dad.'

Sara's house was right up the other end of Eppingham to us, over the motorway bridge, and my dad dropped me off in the car. When we got there he looked at the house and at me as if he wasn't going to let me go.

I opened the door quickly and got out, before he could say anything else about shabby houses.

He leant across the passenger seat, catching the door before I could bang it shut. 'I'll ring you later,' he said again, and he stayed there, watching, as I ran up the path.

Their house was different in the dark. The hall light bulb had gone so you had to rely on the light from the kitchen at one end and the living room at the other to light it. Mostly it was in darkness, as the hall turned a corner between one and the other. Sara's mum's bedroom was at the front, next to the living room, with the front door in between. I'd come in the back door but I followed Sara down the hall to the front door, to hang my coat up on the pegs.

'Where's your mum?' I asked, shivering slightly now I'd taken off my coat.

'Out,' she said. 'Till late. She's gone round a friend's. The boys have gone to get beer. Come upstairs.'

She *was* wearing her jeans. They were tight and very faded and fraying at the backs of the hems. She didn't have her trainers on; I followed her up the stairs looking at her socks – thick woolly grey socks that were too big for her and flopped over her toes as she walked. Socks like a man might wear, like walking socks.

I put my bag beside the spare bed in her room. There was no lampshade on the light bulb and the naked light lit the room bright yellow in the middle and cast eerie shadows in the corners.

'I'm just going to get changed,' Sara said and pulled her jumper off over her head, crackling her hair with the static. Immediately goosebumps shivered over her naked arms. Her skin looked blue-white under the yellow light, transparent almost. She'd got a top out ready on her bed, and I stood by her chest of drawers, fiddling with the things scattered on top while she put it on and buttoned it up.

Then she came over to me and we peered into her mirror together; in the dimness of the room my eyes in all that eyeliner looked completely black, like coals.

I watched as Sara touched up her make-up, doing her own eyeliner in that funny way, and putting on her lipstick, which she did in three parts: top left side, top right side, then straight across the bottom lip. She ground her lips together, rubbing it in, then she checked her teeth for any smudges, rubbing them off with her little finger. When she'd finished I went over to my bag and took out the pink lipstick that she'd given me. Looking back in the mirror again I slicked it on; now *she* was watching *me*. I met her gaze in the mirror and held it; I smiled my best pink smile and Sara smiled back.

'You look nice,' she said.

The heat from the gas fire was making me drowsy, that and the cider. And I was useless at shuffling the cards; every time it was my turn the cards seemed to go everywhere and Sara and I fell about laughing. I'd never played whist before; Glenn was showing me the rules.

'It's not fair,' Rachel said. 'You keep winning because there's two of you.'

'I'm surprised she doesn't lose with Glenn helping her,' Sara said and took a swig from the bottle of cider we were sharing. Then she passed it to me without wiping the top. I put it to my lips straight away so that I could taste her. Sara lay on the floor, propped up on her elbows, watching me.

'No,' Rachel insisted. 'We should all pair up.'

'Oh God,' Sara groaned. 'You two! Can't bear to be parted!' She was still looking at me. I grinned round the bottle at her, holding her stare. There was a message in her eyes; I saw it but couldn't make out what it said.

'Shut up, you.' Rachel prodded Sara in the face with her foot as she got up from the floor by Mark's chair and plonked herself down on his lap. Mark put his arms around her, snuggling his face into her curly hair.

So we played in pairs and it was fun at first but my head felt woozy. We were in a sort of circle: Mark and Rachel in one chair, Glenn in the other with me sitting at his feet holding the cards up for him to see, and Sara and Andy sprawled out on the floor. The cider bottle kept passing back and forth between Sara and me. Glenn peered down over my shoulder to see the cards and I made whatever moves he told me to, but my attention was all on Sara. Every time she passed me the bottle I drank and passed it back again, just to keep up the contact.

Her top had separated from her jeans where she was stretched out. Andy put his hand on her back and touched the naked skin there. Then he moved his hand down and slapped it on her backside. He leant right against her to whisper in her ear and she laughed at what he said. Her laugh sounded coarse, and little nerves in my stomach jarred.

Glenn moved so that I was leaning against the chair,

between his legs. He brushed my hair back from my ear with his fingers to whisper instructions and left his hand resting on my shoulder. Sara stopped passing me the bottle, and used her mouth to kiss Andy instead.

Just before ten-thirty Rachel and Mark left because Rachel had to be home by half past. They let themselves out, but as they opened the back door we heard Mark say, 'Oh! Hello, Mrs Williams!'

'Shit! It's my mum!' Sara darted out into the hall and closed the door behind her. Glenn stubbed out his cigarette then opened the window and stuck the ashtray out on the sill. I stayed sitting on the floor and looked at Andy. He grimaced and shrugged his shoulders, then got up from the floor and sat on the edge of the sofa, skinny elbows propped on skinny knees. Glenn closed the window again and stood, listening, in the middle of the room. Nobody spoke. We were all waiting, though I didn't know what for till it came.

The voices in the hall were muffled. I couldn't make out what they were saying but then I heard Sara crying, 'Mum . . . please . . . Oh, Mum!' It started off pleading but turned to a shout; there was a thump and then another thump and someone muttered something but I don't know what; and then I heard another door opening and Sara crying, 'Mum!' again.

I gripped my hands round my knees. I couldn't bear

to sit there, listening. 'What should I do?' I whispered to Glenn. He shook his head at me, hushing me. He was tense, waiting for what might come next.

They must have been in her mother's room now, just across the hall. We heard a thud as someone bashed into furniture and Sara saying, 'Mum . . . Come on . . .' and then there was the sound of someone crying, an awful, tortured sound like a cat howling in the night.

'Jesus . . .' Glenn put his hand up to his forehead. It was clenched tight in a fist. 'Jesus,' he said again, and went out of the room.

Andy and I sat, staring at each other. I opened my mouth to speak but he put his finger to his lips in a silent hush. We could hear Glenn's voice and Sara's, though not what they were saying, and still that pitiful crying noise.

My leg was going numb. I moved my foot and pins and needles shot up to my knee. I wriggled and waggled my foot but it was no good so I leant forward and rubbed at my leg with my hands. The rasp against the denim was loud in the room; I saw Andy tilt his head more to try and hear what was going on outside the door.

It had gone quiet. After an age the door opened a little and Glenn came in.

'All right, mate?' Andy asked quietly as Glenn sat down on the edge of the other chair, rubbing his hands up and down his thighs.

'Yeah ... Yeah ...' He was watching the door, frowning. It opened wider and Sara came in. Her face was white, totally drained, red mouth clenched into a thin hard line.

I moved over a little so she could sit in the chair. She knocked me with her legs as she sat down and slouched forward with her chin in her hands.

'She all right?' Glenn asked her. Sara nodded and stared at the carpet.

'Look ... I better be going,' Andy said and stood up awkwardly. He was tall, much taller than the rest of us, and seemed even more so now, standing there like he didn't know what to do.

'I'll see you out, mate,' Glenn said. Andy stroked Sara's head as he passed her but she didn't move.

When they'd gone I shuffled over to Sara and put my hand on her thigh to try and comfort her. The muscle in her leg was rock hard. I didn't speak; I couldn't think what to say. She seemed taut as a string, about to snap.

Ages seemed to pass. I heard the back door close and then water clanging through the pipes as Glenn used the bathroom, then his footsteps on the stairs. Then there was no other sound but the fading banging of the plumbing and the gentle hiss of the gas fire.

Suddenly, Sara started to cry. The tension broke out of her body in great sobs and she pressed her face into her hands.

'Sara . . .' I got to my knees to put my arms around her and pulled her to me, so that her head was against my shoulder. Still she kept her hands over her face.

'Sara, shush . . .' I held her like a child, like the most precious thing. She cried with her mouth open and at first I couldn't hear what she was saying, couldn't separate the words from the sobs.

'. . . now what must you think?'

'What?'

'Now what must you think of us – of me?' She pulled away to look at me through bloodshot, black-smudged eyes. It seemed to me that all the pain and anger in the world was painted on her streaky face.

'What do you mean?' I reached for her again but she held herself away.

'Well now you've really seen it all. Great piece of gossip for you.'

'Oh, Sara . . .' Her hands were in her lap now, clawing at each other. I covered them with my own. 'Sara, don't think like that. It doesn't matter. It doesn't make any difference.'

'That's what you say, but I bet you can't wait to get away and tell everyone.'

'Don't say that,' I said, holding on to her hands. 'It's not true. I'm not going to tell anyone.' Her hands were hot and tight in mine. 'It doesn't matter. *You* matter,

Sara. I care about you. I'm your friend. You won't get rid of me that easy.'

Her hands twisted round so that she was holding mine, and then it was my eyes filling with tears.

'Don't you start,' she said and squeezed my hands, 'or we'll never stop.' She sighed and tried to smile but it didn't reach her sad, sad eyes. 'Come on,' she said. 'Let's go to bed.'

Her room was bitterly cold after the poisonous heat of the living room. Sara dragged off her jeans but kept on her socks and knickers and pulled a jumper on over the top she was wearing, and climbed into bed.

She said, 'Get the light, will you?' so I put on my pyjamas and kept my socks on and got into the spare bed. The sheets felt lumpy, as if there were crumbs in there, or hard lumps of fluff. Nerves and the cold sent shivers right through my body and I couldn't imagine ever being warm again. I lay curled on my side, holding my toes to warm then. I breathed in through my nose and out through my mouth, in, out, in, out, to try and calm my body but the shivers still went through me, in hard, random jerks.

Sara was lying on her back, staring at the ceiling. I could just make out the paleness of her face against the covers and the glint of her eye in the darkness. She sighed.

'Are you all right?' I croaked. She seemed to have forgotten I was there.

'Mmm? Yes. It's just my mum. She's worried about the shop. That's why she drinks too much. It's not her fault.'

I'd imagined girly chats and secrets and laughter into the early hours, not this. Sara sighed again and I lay watching her; after a while I couldn't see her eyes any more and then I heard her breathing change to faint snores. *She snores*, I thought. *Wait till I tell her in the morning!* Only it didn't seem particularly funny just then. I listened to the noises of the house creaking and settling and hoped to God that the fire was turned off properly and the electrics were safe.

I thought I'd never sleep. The bed sagged in the middle and every time I moved the quilt would slide one way and the blankets the other. I suppose I must have dozed a bit but I was awake to see the darkness lessen and hear the first cars starting up on the street outside. I felt for my watch beside the bed and strained my eyes to read it. It was only ten past seven. On a Sunday morning. I flopped back down and tucked my nose under the blankets to warm it; they smelt sort of salty.

Sara was hunched up with her back to me. I needed to go to the loo. I thought about waiting till she awoke but then I couldn't bear the embarrassment of bumping into Sara's mother on my way out of the bathroom and having to say, 'Oh hi, I'm Kate, I stayed here last night.'

Sara was fast asleep. I crept past her and out on to the landing. Glenn's door opposite was slightly open but it was pitch-dark in there. I tip-toed down the stairs, quiet as I could, hoping that no one woke, but then I had to crank the handle on the loo several times to flush it and no one would sleep through the noise the pipes made. In the bathroom I washed my hands with hard soap and flicked icy water on to my face. There was a mirror on the door of the bathroom cabinet; I rubbed at it with my sleeve to clear it and then peered at my grey face. I looked awful and I felt awful, that horrid sick feeling that comes from lack of sleep.

I crept back upstairs as fast as I could and closed the bedroom door behind me. Sara groaned into her pillow and rolled over to face me, pulling her duvet and the blanket she'd got covering it up snug around her chin. The remains of last night's make-up were smudged panda-like around her eyes.

'What time is it?' she muttered.

'Don't know. Earlyish. Sorry I woke you.' I padded over and sat on her bed. She tugged her blanket out from under me. 'How come everything didn't slide off your bed in the night?' I asked.

'Because I don't fidget,' she said.

'Yes you do. And you snore,' I said, and shivered. 'It's freezing out here.'

'Well get in then.' She moved over to make room and I snuggled into the warmth of her body. The bed dipped in the middle so we dipped down too with our hips touching. 'God your legs are cold,' she said and her breath smelt buttery.

I didn't see her mother when we got up, or Glenn. I left their house at about ten-thirty, to walk home, and neither of them was up yet. I left Sara in the kitchen, cleaning the floor with an old wet rag tied round a mop and bagging up washing for the launderette.

5

Sara wasn't in school on Monday. I'd have called for her like normal but I was running late and I thought she'd have already gone on ahead. When I got to school the bell had gone and most people had gone in; I hurried across the playground with the other stragglers and ran all the way up the stairs and into tutorial.

She wasn't there.

The disappointment was amazing. I'd *so* expected her to be there. I was dying to speak to her; I hadn't stopped thinking about her all day Sunday and half Sunday night and I wanted to talk about it all; about her, about her mum and the money – about the whole situation. There was so much to talk about. I felt we were real, deep friends now, more than that. As if Sara was a tin box and I'd got the top off and seen what was inside.

I sat at my place and waited for Sara to come in late and she didn't. On the way out of registration Juliet looked at me till she caught my eye, then smirked and looked away again. She had *Now who are you going to hang around with?* written all over her smug little face.

In Art I still half-hoped that Sara might come in late but she didn't, so I thought I'd go and find Glenn at break and ask him what was wrong. But I couldn't find Glenn, either. I stood by the main building, scanning the whole playground, but I couldn't see him anywhere. I took my time looking, because I had nothing else to do. I could see Juliet, Hanna and Melanie sitting in our old spot at the far side of the quiet area; no way was I going to go and hang around by them.

Glenn definitely wasn't in the playground so I wandered around the pathways at the back of the school, past the Science block and the canteen, looking for him there. We weren't supposed to go around there at break, but we all did. I'd just about given up when I saw Andy and Mark and a couple of other boys from Year Eleven mucking around by the sports block, kicking someone's bag between them as if it was a football.

'All right, Kate?' Andy said when I went up to him, and they stopped kicking that bag for a second.

'Where's Glenn?' I asked, and Andy grinned, and so did a couple of the other boys. I could feel myself going red. 'I wanted to ask him why Sara's not here,' I said.

'Oh right,' Andy said, like he didn't believe me. He pushed his floppy yellow hair back from his face. 'Don't know where he is. Haven't seen him today. But if I do I'll tell him you were looking for him, OK?'

'I was looking for Sara,' I said.

'Right,' Andy said again, still grinning.

* * *

At lunchtime I went round to their house. Normally I went straight round the back but that was when Sara knew I was coming; today I went to the front door. I couldn't see anything through the little squares of glass and the noise in the street made it impossible to hear anybody inside. There was no bell. Spiders' webs shrouded the knocker and came away on my fingers as I rapped on the door. There was no response at first and I knocked again, then I heard Sara mutter, 'Fucking door, always sticks,' and the door shook and was rattled and then jerked open.

Sara peered round. Her eyes were red from crying and she looked awful. She stared at me, blank-faced for a moment, as if she didn't even know me.

'Sara? I wondered where you were, what was wrong . . .'

'Come in.'

She held the door back and I went into the gloom. The house smelt damp at the best of times but today there was something else, as if the air was disturbed. She wasn't pleased to see me, I could tell. I stood in the hall while she tried to close the door. Eventually she kicked it and snapped, 'Fucking door. It never works, you know it doesn't work,' and burst out into tears.

'Sara . . .' I reached out to her but she pushed past me. The door to her mother's bedroom was open; she went in and I followed her. Glenn was sitting on the floor, searching through the contents of a drawer. The other drawers in the chest were open, and papers and all sorts were strewn everywhere. Glenn ferreted through, flinging scraps of paper into the air like bursts of confetti. He didn't even look up at me.

Sara sat on the bed, crying as if she'd been crying for so long that she'd given up trying to stop. Mean tears crawled slowly out of her eyes and she made a constant kind of groaning noise. She pulled out the drawer of the bedside table and tipped it out on to the bed. She put her hands into the pile and began turning it over.

I thought her mum must have died.

'What's wrong?'

No one answered me. Glenn didn't even seem to know I was there and Sara was hunched over letters and bills and things. Leaning forward was making her nose run; she kept snorting; it gurgled horribly and the drip kept coming back. I couldn't stand to watch. I walked down the hall to get some loo paper from the toilet for her. The living room door was open and in there it looked like burglars had turned the place over, except, of course, there was nothing to steal.

When I came back into the bedroom I sat beside Sara and put the tissue into her hand. She wiped it across her nose and shuddered.

'What's happened? What are you looking for?' I touched her arm, half-expecting her to shake me off. She was wearing the jumper she'd slept in on Saturday night. Bits of fluff from her bed stuck to it.

'Money. We're looking for money. And there isn't any.'

'I'm going for a fag,' Glenn said and got up from the mess on the floor.

He kicked the chest of drawers and Sara snapped, 'Yes, that's it. Just give up, why don't you?'

He stopped at the door and turned round. 'I am not giving up, Sara, I am going for a fag. I will be five minutes. OK?'

Sara glared back at him but as soon as he'd gone her face just crumpled and she sat sobbing among the heaps of discarded junk. 'Look at it all!' She swept a pile of old letters off the bed with her hand. 'We've missed the rent and we'll lose the house if we don't find the money to pay it. We've been searching all morning. Somewhere there's a thousand pounds in premium bonds but we don't know where it was put when we moved. It could be anywhere.' Her voice rose to a wail. 'We don't know if its here or at the shop. My mum's there now looking but she's in enough of a state because she owes the bank already and even if we do find the money it's not nearly enough and we'll probably lose the house *and* the shop . . .'

She rubbed the tissue across her nose. She'd screwed it into a tight ball and it didn't do much good.

'Listen,' I said. 'It must be here somewhere. Let me help too. Where have you looked so far?'

'Everywhere,' she sobbed, then contradicted herself by saying, 'We've still got the cases under the bed to go through and then there's all the boxes under the stairs . . . Anyway, it's not your problem. You better get back to school.'

'I've got ages yet,' I said. 'I'm not leaving you like this.'

When Glenn came back, Sara and I were pulling one of the cases out from under the bed. It weighed a ton and he helped us lift it up on to the bed so that he had room on the floor to go through the other one. Sara and I sat at opposite sides of the bed, with the case split horizontally between us, and delved through old fabric cuttings and brochures and household bills. Most of it should have gone in the bin but we just transferred it from one side of the case to the other.

I forgot that this was *serious*. Sara had stopped crying and was sorting through the things in the bottom of the wardrobe, saying things like *If she wasn't so dozy we wouldn't be in this mess* and *Stupid fucking house, don't know where anything is.*

'It's here somewhere, it's got to be,' Glenn said. It was like a race, to see who would find it first.

I didn't even know what a premium bond looked like.

Glenn found it.

He said, 'Hang on!' and ripped open a little brown envelope filled with over-sized Monopoly money.

'*Yes!*' I bounced down from the bed and grabbed at the envelope with him.

'Are you sure?' Sara came round from the other side of the bed. Her voice sounded tight. 'How much is there?'

The bonds were in hundred pounds. Glenn began to count them out. I counted with him.

Sara bent down and snatched them from our hands. 'This isn't a fucking game, you know!' she snapped, then she kicked her way through all that stuff and out of the room.

She was in her room, sitting on her bed. When I opened the door she raised her head just enough to glare at me then turned away again, eyes down, fingers fiddling with the bobbles on her jumper.

'I'm sorry,' I said to her back.

She jumped round again, glaring at me, eyes still red from tears. 'You just haven't got a clue, have you? You come round here in your poncy clothes—' She looked me up and down, flicked a hand out, dismissing me. 'What is it with you?' she demanded, so *angry*. 'Do you get your kicks snooping round other people's houses, or what?'

'Sara, I'm sorry—'

'Oh get lost,' she snapped. She started picking the fluff off the bottom of her jumper now, eyes down, bony white fingers agitated, busy.

'Sara—' I pleaded, but it was like talking to a wall. She'd shut me out totally.

'I said get lost,' she repeated, and I could not believe how cold she had become.

I stood outside their house, crying my eyes out. I couldn't bear to just go away and I thought she'd come out after me, in a little while. But she didn't, and eventually I went back to school – late, very late. I didn't go into English, I went into the loos instead and rubbed at my face with a paper towel. I'd say I was sick or something, or had a headache. I couldn't face Juliet and the others; I didn't want to see anyone. I couldn't believe Sara could turn on me like that, after Saturday night.

They weren't in school on Tuesday, either. I hung around on my own at break because I couldn't bear to speak to anyone, and at lunchtime I went to the rec at the end of their road and sat on a bench, just inside the gate. I could see quite a way up the street from there, though not quite as far as their house. I sat there for the whole hour, just staring up the road, in case Sara came out, in case I should see her.

I went back to that bench after school. Normally there'd be quite a few kids hanging around by the rec after school but it was a miserable dark day and the clouds were closing in, bringing drizzle, that heavy persistent drizzle that gets you soaked right through to the skin, and no one hung about for long. I wanted to go round to their house but I was too scared, so I sat there, huddled into my jacket and shivering, wishing for Sara to come to me, for her to appear suddenly, striding up the street towards me, all loving smiles and forgiveness.

She didn't, of course.

I was sitting there getting slowly soaked as the drizzle turned to rain, and feeling thoroughly sorry for myself, when Andy skidded to a halt at the rec gates on his bicycle, tyres crunching noisily on the wet gravel. I didn't realize it was him at first; he'd got the hood of his sweatshirt pulled right up over his face, hiding him from the rain.

'Kate?' he called from the gate. 'What you doing?'

'Nothing.' I shrugged when I recognized his voice, and tried to smile, embarrassed at being caught like that, sitting in the rain on my own like some nutter.

'Are you coming round Sara's?' He pushed his hood back, flinching as the rain hit his face.

'I can't.' I stood up, stuffing my hands deep in my pockets to still them from shaking with the cold. I curled them into cosy fists, tight, and held them that way for comfort.

'Why? What's up?' Andy yelled and I walked over to him, blinking the rain out of my eyes.

'Sara's annoyed with me,' I said and my throat burnt; I blinked harder against the weather and tightened my fists even more, digging my nails into my hands.

'Don't be daft,' Andy said. 'Come with me if you're worried. I'm going round there now.'

'No.' I shook my head and felt the tears rise; shook it harder to clear them. 'I don't think so.'

He shrugged and rode off. It's that simple for boys: do it or don't. There's no epic *Shall I?* or *Shan't I?* No endless searching in between.

I stayed there a while longer till there was no one left coming past from school and the light was beginning to dip. I walked past her house then, going home that way. The light was on in the living room and there were two bikes propped against the side wall. If I was a real friend I'd be in there, with them. If I was a real friend I wouldn't think twice about walking up to the door, I'd know Sara would be glad to see me, I'd say *Hi* and *Sorry* and that would be that.

If I was a real friend I wouldn't have behaved like such a tourist in the first place.

By Wednesday morning I was desperate to make it up with her.

She came in late to tutorial. Mrs Rupert just said, 'Sit

down, Sara,' quietly, without even asking why she was late, or where she'd been. It was clear that *allowances* were being made, that Sara had *special circumstances*. I knew this and so did everybody else and Sara must have hated us knowing. She didn't look at me and she sat with her back half-turned to me, hunched over her bag.

We had English after tutorial. As soon as the bell rang for us to go, Sara grabbed up her bag and went on ahead, making it very clear that she didn't want to talk to me. I trailed along behind her to the classroom, and as I went to sit at my desk I heard Ruth and Juliet talking about her. They were sitting at their desks already, leaning towards each other across the gap and hunched up close like a pair of scheming witches.

'She's obviously dirt poor,' Ruth whispered; a stage whisper, just loud enough so that anyone who wanted to could hear. She was sitting with her back to me and hadn't seen me come in. '*And* I heard that her mother's an alcoholic . . .'

Juliet knew I was there. I saw her eyes flick up and flick down again. 'Well that's no excuse,' she said. She didn't bother whispering; it was obvious that she wanted me to hear. 'She's just a tart, hanging around with her brother's friends all the time, and Kate'll end up just like her if she's not careful.'

They shut up as I sat down, and Juliet turned her back to me, all smug with self-righteousness. I half-expected her to huff and toss her hair, she was that ridiculous. Maybe she did; I don't remember now. But I do remember the way she started tearing up little bits of paper straight away and frantically scribbling, shoulder hunched against me, using her arm to hide what she wrote. The notes went back and forth all lesson. I could imagine what they said, but I was too miserable to care.

At break Sara went straight over to Glenn and Andy in the playground. I stood by the main doors, watching them. I wondered what she'd told them about me. They must have noticed that I wasn't around any more, they must have asked her why. Sara looked as if she didn't care, though. She was laughing and talking with them as if nothing was wrong at all. Like she'd cut me out of her life and that was that: over. I couldn't stand it.

We were in different classes for Maths and at lunchtime she must have gone off home with Glenn so I didn't see her again until Art, after lunch.

She tried to ignore me, staring down at her paper as if she cared what her drawing turned out like. She held her pencil really tight, in a sort of cack-handed way, the way boys sometimes do when they're young. No wonder she was so awful at Art. She went over and over the same bit of her drawing holding that pencil as if it was some creature that might escape at any moment. Her picture was a mass of hard, dark lines.

I watched her with my heart racing. She wasn't going to look up; she wasn't going to make this any easier for me. Everything about her was hostile. There were hollows in her cheeks where she'd got her teeth clamped so hard together and her chin was jutting out, lips tight. She'd hunched up one shoulder and her head was tilted to that side, leaving the other side of her neck stretched out and exposed.

'Sara,' I said at last. 'I'm really sorry. Please talk to me.'

She tilted her head the other way and looked at me at last. Her eyes were cold and guarded.

'I'm really sorry,' I said again, and it came out like a plea, like so many excuses. 'I didn't mean to upset you . . . I was just so glad we found the money—'

'You just don't get it, do you?' she said, shaking her head as she spoke. 'A thousand pounds isn't going to pay the rent, pay the bills, save the shop. A thousand pounds isn't going to go very far – and what do we do then? Where does the next thousand come from? And what am I supposed to tell my mum every time another bill comes in and we run out of food?'

'Surely your dad—'

'Oh leave him out of it. At the moment we're surviving on Glenn's paper round and my thirty pounds from the greengrocer's. Oh, and handouts from Uncle fucking Ron. Not much, is it?'

Sara glared at me as if waiting for an answer – but what could I say? I held her stare but I could feel the tears building up in my eyes.

'Oh for God's sake,' Sara snapped. 'I don't need this.'

I had a hundred pounds left over from my birthday last year, that I still hadn't spent. I'd kept it stuffed in my jewellery box, waiting to see if I'd get any more money for Christmas. I'd been thinking of buying a suede jacket. Well I supposed I could live without a suede jacket, and Mum and Dad needn't know the money had gone. There was another forty-eight pounds fifty-eight pence in my money box and I still had seven pounds of my pocket money left. Not much really but it seemed like a lot when I stuffed notes and coins into my purse.

I left home early in the morning and went to Sara's house before school. Glenn let me into the kitchen. He was stuffing toast into his mouth. 'Sara's upstairs,' he mumbled. 'Go on up.'

I knew I was doing the right thing. I was just so glad to have a reason to be in that house again. Heaven, for me, will smell of burnt toast, damp corners and gas.

I called her name as I ran up the stairs. She was standing by the dressing table, doing her eyes. She put the mascara down as I came in, and turned around. She wasn't in the least pleased to see me.

'Glenn told me to come up,' I said, rather unnecessarily. 'I wanted to see you before school.'

'Well you've seen me now,' she said in that cold, blank voice. Then she went over to the bed, dug her trainers out from under it and sat down to put them on.

I took the purse out from my bag and sat down next to her.

'This is for you.' I tipped the money out on to the bed between us. 'There's one hundred and fifty-five pounds. It's not much but I thought it would help . . .'

'Where did you get it?' she snapped.

'It's mine,' I said. 'It's my birthday money and some other money I had.'

'And how am I supposed to pay you back?' Sarcasm edged her words; this wasn't going how I'd planned.

'I don't want you to pay me back. I just want you to have it.'

The money lay in a heap between us, horribly embarrassing suddenly.

'Look, Sara,' I said, 'you need it, I don't. Take it.'

'I don't need your charity.'

Heat swept across my head, burning my ears. 'Do you know what, Sara?' I shouted at her, jumping up from the bed. 'You're a snob. You think I'm a snob but you're wrong. It's you who's the snob – no, you're worse than that. You're an *inverted* snob.'

I left Sara and the money where they were and ran

back down the stairs. Glenn said, 'Hey – what's wrong?' as I slammed through the kitchen, but I couldn't speak, couldn't stop till I was halfway up the street. I wanted to kick something. There was no pleasing her. It was all one way, all one long, hard slog.

The anger lasted all day. I didn't even look at Sara in class. I knew if I spoke to her I'd say something else I'd regret. So I avoided her all day, and the next too. But then when I was coming out of school on Friday afternoon I saw her walking out the gates on her own. It had turned bitterly cold and her shoulders were braced against the wind. Sara didn't have a coat; she wore an old denim jacket that she'd pinched from her brother. She looked so forlorn. My anger just vanished and I ached for her again.

6

Sara worked at the greengrocer's in the High Street on Saturday mornings. I walked down there straight after breakfast. I stood out the front, by the crates of fruit, watching her throw carrots and potatoes and apples into brown paper bags and count out change. She was wearing fingerless gloves and had a blue woollen hat pulled down low on her head and her nose was pink with the cold. When she'd filled a bag she flipped it over in her hands and twisted the corners closed, the way the greengrocer did.

They were busy first thing and I ended up having to wait back out on the pavement till the queue eased off. I thought Sara would pretend not to have seen me but she didn't. As soon as it quietened down a bit she came over to me.

'You can come in, you know,' she said, rubbing her fingertips together to warm them. 'You don't have to hide out there among the oranges.'

'Sara, listen,' I said, talking fast in case she walked off again, without hearing me out, 'I've got to talk to you. I'm really, really sorry, honestly—'

'Yeah, well. Forget it.' She put her hands up to her

face now, cupping them over her nose and mouth and blowing slowly into them to try and warm her nose up.

'Are we still friends?'

'Yeah. Course we are.' The words were muffled behind her hands. She smiled then. I couldn't see her mouth because it was hidden by her hands but her cheeks lifted slightly and so did the corners of her eyes. The colour of those eyes brightened, like the sea when it's lit by the sun. I felt such relief I could have cried.

The greengrocer came in from the back of the shop then, with a bag of potatoes balanced on one shoulder.

'I can't talk now,' Sara said. 'Come back for me later. I get off at one.'

I wanted to do something special to celebrate. I wanted to buy chocolates or flowers, but I hardly had any money left so I went to the newsagent and spent my fifty eight pence on cheap sweets meant for little kids: fizzy chews and gummy cola bottles and lollipops that turn your tongue blue.

At one o'clock I was there at the greengrocer's waiting for Sara, and we walked back through the rec to her house, arms linked together, gorging ourselves.

We went into the kitchen and I threw myself down on to one of the chairs, clutching at my stomach. 'Urgh

. . . I so feel sick,' I groaned. 'I can't believe I've just had sweets for lunch.'

'You've got no stamina.' Sara filled the kettle and put it on the hob to boil, sloshing water out of the spout and on to the floor as she did so. It took three matches to light the gas. As each one burnt up towards the end she turned her fingers in a graceful arc to avoid the flame, then with the same fingers flicked the blackened stick at the sink. Twice she missed. Twice the matches fell to the floor and crumbled and dissolved black on the wet lino. There were loads of dead match ends down there, scattered around the edges and in the corner beside the sink. They must get through millions every day. Then she opened the door into the hall; it was dark out there, even in daytime. 'Glenn,' she yelled into the silence, then again even louder, 'Glenn! Where are you?'

The floorboards above creaked and Sara sniggered at me, hand over her mouth, all conspiratorial. We could hear Glenn stumbling down the stairs and we watched the open doorway till he came into view, shuffling along the hall, still doing up his jeans. His hair was sticking up in tufts and he squinted as he came into the kitchen, blinking his eyes as the light hit them.

'What's the matter?' he asked, green eyes pale, blurry.

'Nothing,' Sara said sweetly. 'Just wondered if you want a cup of tea.'

'What? Is that all? I was asleep . . .'

'Lazy bastard.' Sara grinned at me.

'I don't think so,' he said. 'I'd only just gone back to bed. I've been up delivering papers since six o'bloody clock.' He rubbed his hands through his hair. He had hair like Sara's, only a boy's version: the same colour but thicker, coarser. It was sticking up where he'd ruffled it.

'So? I've been up since the crack of dawn too,' Sara quipped. 'Anyway, I thought Kate might like to see how delightful you look when you've just woken up.'

Glenn coloured at this, ever so slightly. I probably wouldn't have even noticed but Sara pointed at his face and said, 'Ha-ha!'

'Shut up, Sara.' He pulled out the chair opposite me and sat down sideways, legs stretched out. He had woolly socks on his feet, like Sara sometimes wore. She must steal his, I supposed. There was a hole in the left one so big that two of his toes were poking right through. 'I might as well have that tea then, now that I'm up,' he said, yawning as he spoke.

'Well don't just sit there getting in the way,' Sara said, kicking his feet out the way as she turned to make the tea. 'Make yourself useful. Get your fags out.'

'God, Kate, does she nag you like this?' Glenn asked, rolling his eyes at me and I laughed.

'Yes,' I said, and joy bubbled up inside me. I was just so happy to be there again. And so glad that everything was all right after all.

Glenn leant forwards in his chair, reaching behind him to pull a cigarette packet from his back pocket. The packet was squashed at one end, where he'd been sitting on it. 'You do it,' he said, pushing it across the table to me. 'I'm still half-asleep.'

The cigarettes were bent slightly; I took out three, straightening them with my fingers. 'Matches, please, Sara,' I called and she tossed them over her shoulder to me with one hand as she spooned sugar into tea with the other. She was way off mark; I had to jump up, quick, to catch them in mid-air before they hit the wall. I lit three in turn, using one match; I was getting pretty good at this, by now. I handed Glenn his and then puffed alternately on Sara's and mine till she was ready to take one.

When the tea was made, Sara sat down on the other chair and we stayed there all afternoon talking and smoking and drinking tea till the cigarettes ran out. We took it in turns to refill the kettle and put it back on to boil, and the handle got so hot eventually that we had to hold a cloth round it to lift it. It grew dark outside and the window was black and fogged up with steam from the kettle; every now and then a drip would form at the top and start to run down, making little rivers on the glass. We were all so cosy, warmed by smoke and gas and steam.

I didn't want to go. I wanted to stay there forever, just as we were. I wanted time frozen, I wanted us frozen, our thoughts and our smiles and the sounds of our voices. Frozen, captured, never to be lost.

You know how it is when you are so happy that you feel like you are being stretched inside, so much that it almost hurts? Like elastic, stretched and stretched till it is about to tear, you just know it could tear at any moment. That is how I felt; stretched out, taut inside. One wrong move and it would all snap back into nothing.

I kept looking at the clock up on the wall and watching the long hand clicking on round. I wished I could stop it. I wished I could stop time.

Suddenly my phone started ringing, breaking into our idyll. I knew it would be my mum, chasing up on me. I took it out of my jacket pocket and turned it off, without answering.

'I'll walk with you some of the way if you like,' Sara said as I slowly stood up, pulling on my jacket, doing it up tight, unwilling to leave.

Just as Sara opened the back door Glenn said, as if he'd been thinking about it for a while, 'I'm glad you two have made it up. It's good you coming round here, Kate.'

* * *

The cold hit us straight away like a slap in the face. Instantly we drew together and Sara stuck her arm through mine, huddling close. It's horrible going out into the cold when you've been so still and warm and cosy. I held on to Sara's arm through the over-large sleeve of her denim jacket, hugging it tight, and I could feel her body shivering against mine.

She walked with me all the way to the motorway bridge, stopping at the top. Then she dropped her arm down from mine and we both started shivering again, away from each other's warmth.

'Right, then,' she said, teeth chattering over the words. 'I'll see you on Monday.'

'I'll call for you,' I said. I didn't want to leave her.

'Make it early,' she said, turning away from me, hands plunged deep into her pockets. 'Bye, then.'

I stayed standing there and Sara looked back over her shoulder at me, laughing. 'Well go on, then,' she called. But I didn't go on, and she didn't look back again. She hunched up her shoulders and walked fast, head bent into the wind. I stood at the the top of the bridge and watched her little body getting smaller in the distance.

'Where've you been?' my mum demanded as soon as I let myself in, taking off my shoes and jacket in the back porch and going through to the kitchen. She was sitting at the table with some papers in front of her and an old towel around her shoulders. Her wet black hair was squashed up under a clear plastic shower cap, being blackened further. She did this every five weeks or so, to hide those unwanted greys.

'At Sara's,' I said.

'I expected you home ages ago,' she said, peering at me through glasses perched precariously low on her ears and nose so as not to get dye on the frame. 'And I tried to phone you.'

'Sorry,' I lied. 'Battery went flat.'

'What is the point in my buying you a phone if you don't keep it charged up? And I'm sure Sara has a phone you could use, doesn't she?' Suddenly she wrinkled her nose, and stared at me harder. 'What's that smell?'

'All I can smell is your hair dye.'

'Have you been smoking?' she barked, voice sharp with suspicion.

'No,' I replied, hurt, outraged. And then I said, as soon as I thought of it, 'They were having a bonfire at Sara's. Her brother had cleared up all the leaves and stuff from the garden. That's why I'm late. Sara's mum made us hot dogs. Sorry.' I sniffed at my jumper. 'My clothes probably stink.'

'Well make sure you ring next time if you're going to

be late, Kate,' my mum said, looking at her watch now to check the timing of her hair.

'Sorry,' I said again – and that's how easy it was, lying to my parents.

I was at Sara's really early on Monday morning, knocking on the back door. She was in the kitchen; I could see her shadow through the glass of the door, moving about.

'Jesus, you're keen,' she said as I came in. 'It's not even half past eight yet.' She was making toast but she'd burnt it; the sink and the little bit of surface around it were covered in tiny black crumbs where she'd scraped the burnt bits off. She used the same knife to put the spread on, adding to the crumbs already in the tub.

She took the toast upstairs with her and I came up too, and sat on her bed, watching her rush around getting ready. Sara always wore make-up, always. She put it on now, trying to eat the toast at the same time. She held her little mirror up with one hand while the other hand alternated between her mascara wand and the toast. She didn't put the mascara wand back in its tube when she picked up the toast to bite it, she put it down on the plate, balancing it on the edge, trying to save time. But then the mascara would dry up on the wand and she'd have to stick it back in the tube after all, and pump it up and down to get it covered again. She looked at herself when she'd finished, standing back from her chest of drawers and looking in the mirror above it. She looked at herself in a very critical way, turning to one side and then the other, frowning at what she saw. I wondered what she was seeing, and what it was that she was searching for, that could make her look so serious.

We walked to school together arm in arm, in a hurry now, even though I'd got to her house so early. We didn't have much time to talk after all, but when we were walking to the Art block after registration, Sara said, as if it was a great honour, 'My brother fancies you.'

I felt the heat rush into my face. 'No he doesn't,' I said back, instantly annoyed. I wanted to talk about us, not Glenn. I didn't want to hear this.

She stopped and looked at me. 'What's the matter, don't you like him?' Now *she* sounded annoyed, defensive.

'Of course I like him,' I said, pacifying her. 'It's just—'

'He said you're really pretty.' She said it like a challenge. She was looking at me like it was a challenge. My heart began to thud slow and hard.

'Of course I like him,' I said again.

She stood in front of me with her eyes narrowed and I thought everything that I was feeling must be there on my face for her to see, but after a few seconds she smiled and shoved me with her arm. 'It's all right, Miss Innocent,' she said, walking on again. 'I know what you're worried about. Don't worry. He thinks you're sweet. Anyway you'll see him at lunchtime. Him and Andy are coming back today.'

I sat in Art, concentrating on my drawing, concentrating on my thoughts. Sara sat opposite me, with the vase we were drawing on the desk between us. Every time I looked up at the vase I also looked at Sara. She'd got charcoal all over her hands, and on her nose too where she'd rubbed at it. I had the sense of something slipping now, out of my control. I couldn't give a damn about Sara's brother but I would die rather than make her angry again.

At lunchtime I met her at the gates. We crossed the road and walked round the corner, out of sight of the school, then she lit a cigarette and we shared it, two puffs each.

'Relax,' she said. 'He won't eat you.'

'Oh Sara, how do you know he fancies me, anyway?' I spoke quickly, gabbling over the words, clutching for a way out. 'He probably just likes me because I'm your friend. He's probably just being nice.'

But there was no way out. Sara stuck her arm through mine and handed me the cigarette. '*He's probably just being nice,*' she mimicked, laughing at me. 'You do crease me up.'

I sat at the kitchen table with Andy next to me and Glenn opposite while Sara made toast and tea. When that was ready Sara sat down on Andy's lap, lit a cigarette off his, and leant forward with her elbows on the table. I smiled and said yes and no and not much else, and I watched Sara with Glenn and Sara with Andy and saw how easy she was with both of them.

After she told me she was 'seeing' Andy I looked up 'see' in the dictionary. Among other things it said to discern mentally; to understand; to watch; be a spectator. It also said to recognize as acceptable and to observe without interfering. Most of those things applied to me and Sara, and if they didn't yet I was sure they would soon. How could the things that described me describe Andy too?

'God, you've got a bony arse,' Andy said, and tried to push her off.

'Shut your mouth,' Sara said and pushed herself down on him harder. His hands were resting on her thighs. Resting, as if they were used to being there.

They left before us. Sara piled cups into the sink and said, 'Well?'

'Well what?' I asked, playing thick.

'Well, what about Glenn?' she persisted, wiping her

hands dry on her skirt and picking up her jacket, ready to go now.

'What about him?' I spoke dismissively, hoping she'd just drop the subject. 'He doesn't fancy me.'

'You're such an innocent,' she said, all knowing smiles.

7

'Doesn't Sara's mother mind you being round there all the time?'

She'd only been in ten minutes, my mum, and straight away pulled a pinny on over her suit and got on with the chopping. I helped her, a bit, and pinched things off the board, bits of carrot and celery, careful not to lose my fingers under her knife.

'No,' I said, munching on carrot. 'She works a lot. It's nice for Sara to have someone round.'

'Why don't you bring Sara here?' she asked, slapping my hand away.

'Why?' I asked back, playing for time.

It was a ritual, every Friday night, big dinner night. On Wednesdays Mum worked late, counselling the unfortunates, the recently bereaved or recently dumped, and Thursday night was her badminton night. So on Friday she felt the need to be homely, to buy up the supermarket then to cook for us, and catch up and ask a million questions.

'Well you're always out, always at her house,' she said, turning the knife over and using the blunt edge to sweep the chopped stuff on to a plate, making room for more. 'Why don't you both come here?'

'There's no point,' I said. 'She lives on the way home from school. We could hardly come all the way here – then she'd have to go all the way back again.'

'What about Saturdays, then?' she persisted, starting on the onions. 'Why doesn't she come here for a change?' She stopped chopping a moment and looked at me, at the same time pushing her hair back from her face with her clean hand. Onion was making her eyes smart and she blinked quickly, reddening them more.

'Well she works Saturday mornings and her mum's out Saturday nights.' I swiped a piece of mushroom from the plate and bit at it as I spoke. 'And sometimes her cousin Rachel comes round too; she only lives up the road. And we can have the TV to ourselves and watch DVDs,' I lied. 'We couldn't do that here with you here too, could we?' She didn't look convinced, so I wheedled up to her, gave her my sweetest look and fiddled with the pocket on the front of her apron. 'Oh come on, Mum . . . You don't mind me going round there, do you?'

'No of course not, darling.' She smiled at me, pink eyes watering, then bent back down to her vegetables. 'It's just we don't seem to see much of you these days.'

I lay in the bath, rocking gently up and down so that the water sloshed over my body like waves. We had a big bath and I could stretch out almost full length, with just my neck and head resting up at the end. I'd only half-filled the bath, to start with. I always did this, so that I could stay in there for ages and just keep topping it up from the hot tap when the water started to cool, and then it would end up deep, up to my shoulders.

I lowered my body down and then raised it again so the water ran off my tummy but stayed in my belly button, making a tiny dark well. I'd done this since I was little. I used to have some little plastic frogs that I liked to balance on my stomach, around my belly button, and pretend they were drinking from the well. The frogs were long gone but I still liked to do the same things, still liked to fill up that well and then tilt to the side, emptying it out.

Then I bent my knees up and slunk down further into the water, all the time looking down at myself, at the landscape that was me. It was a very lunar landscape, very plain, very lean. My breasts were the first thing, small humps, not even hills, then my ribs ran down into the valley of my stomach, submerged under the sea, and finally my legs rose up out of the water like the highest mountains, the steepest cliffs at the end of this desolate plain.

I had hair, down there. I had it under my armpits too but I shaved that off with a plastic razor, scraping it dry over my skin in the mornings when I remembered. But down there it grew free, unwelcome. Of course I knew that we all had it at our age but I never saw it on the other girls, never saw any of them naked, not even after PE, as the school showers had packed up yonks ago and never been repaired. So I didn't know what anyone else looked like down there and to me that hair looked alien, frightening, sticking out of my smooth skin in jet black tufts.

I lay there looking at my body and feeling as detached from it as I always did. I lifted my hands, disturbing the water, and placed them on my stomach. Then I trailed them, one at a time, up over my ribs to my breasts. I thought about Glenn as I did this, and tried to imagine him fancying me. I closed my eyes and pretended my hands were his hands on me, and I wriggled about a bit in the water to try and get the right effect. My nipples hardened under my fingers, but that was just a reflex; I had no real feeling in my skin. The water splashed about and I wriggled some more but my body was cold like a fish, there was no warmth at all. The heat was all in my mind and there it burnt, but it was Sara it burnt for. Not Glenn.

'Relax,' Glenn whispered as he kissed my ear. 'You're all tense.'

I was sitting on his lap. I'd been there since my dad phoned at ten o'clock. Before that I'd been sitting on the floor, but when I came back in from the hall Glenn grabbed my hand and pulled me down on to his lap. Mark and Rachel had already left, to go for a walk. Sara and Andy were stretched out full length on the sofa, kissing. We'd played cards again earlier, in pairs. Glenn had leant up next to me, taking cards from my hands, then resting his hand on my back.

He was Sara's gift; I had to keep telling myself that. Gift means offering and offering means sacrifice. I remembered my dad telling me once that in certain cultures it is considered the greatest offence to refuse a gift . . . and, depending on the nature of the gift, the one receiving it might be the one to make the sacrifice, might even *be* the sacrifice . . .

'Relax,' Glenn said again. He kissed my neck, little kisses down into the collar of my shirt. His breath made goosepimples spread down my arms.

He shifted me round on his knee so that he could kiss my mouth. I'd never kissed a boy before; his tongue felt huge and tasted of beer. He leant over me, pushing me back over the arm of the chair. I thought I would suffocate, but then he began to kiss my neck again. His fingers were drawing circles on my ribs; they crept up and began to undo my buttons. Panic made me whimper and nudge at his head with my face. He half-looked up at me but his eyes were almost closed and he kissed me again, groaning into my mouth. I wanted to push him off but I couldn't. He was Sara's brother.

I could hear Sara and Andy moving on the sofa; my ears strained for every whisper, every crackle of clothing. Then I heard Sara whine, 'Oh Andy!' and I pulled my face away from Glenn's just as Andy said, 'Glenn. What time is it?'

Glenn took his hand out of my top to look at his watch. 'Nearly eleven.' He sat up and I fell back against the arm of the chair. I did up my buttons before anyone could see.

'Switch the telly on then,' Andy said. He was still sprawled out on the sofa but Sara sat up. Her hair was all messed up and she folded her arms like a cross child.

'Oh for God's sake!' she snapped. 'You're not going to watch football now.'

Glenn reached round me to turn on the TV and I sat up and caught Sara's eye.

'Well if you two are going to be so boring, we're going to bed,' she said, and picked up the cider bottle. 'And we're taking this with us.'

Suddenly it all seemed just too hilarious. I fell back on to Sara's bed and screeched with laughter. I laughed so much it hurt my tummy and made tears run out the corners of my eyes. I laughed so much that it made Sara laugh too and she sat down on the bed beside me.

'Oh Sara!' I gasped. 'What timing! Thank God for football!'

'You're drunk.'

'No I'm not. But I soon will be.' I rolled over and took the cider bottle from her, but drinking lying down made me cough so I sat up and kicked my legs under her duvet.

'This is my bed,' Sara said, trying to shove me off.

'Well I'm sleeping in it tonight,' I said.

'No you're not.'

'Yes I am.'

'Well budge over then,' she said, pushing at me with her body. 'I'm not sleeping in the other bed. Our old cat peed on it before it died.'

'Oh now you tell me.'

'Move over then. And stop hogging the cider.' She wriggled her legs out of her jeans and flung them across the room at the other bed, so I did the same.

'What do you think of my brother then?' she asked.

'He's all right.'

'All right? What's that supposed to mean? I saw you snogging him.' She sighed suddenly and lay down, looking at the ceiling. I lay down too, and looked at her. 'Andy's a prick. He only cares about football. Mark's much nicer. Rachel's lucky.'

She flipped her head round to look at me. 'I was seeing Mark, before he met Rachel,' she said. 'But it wasn't serious. And when he met Rachel they fell in love straight away. I'm really pleased. Rachel deserves to be happy, after the way her step-dad treats her and everything.'

When she spoke her breath warmed my nose. In the shadowy light her eyes looked so beautiful it seemed impossible that they could be used for something so mundane as seeing. It seemed impossible that they could have a purpose at all. So close, I could see the little lines of her irises fanning out from her pupils like segments, like the tiny lines in a grape, cut in half. Long ago, back in the Infants', we collected marbles. We didn't play with them much, just collected them, the most beautiful ones we could find. I had one that was green. It looked green all through at first till you really stared at it and then you noticed the amber flecks flaring out from deep, deep down, almost hidden behind the green. I remembered that marble; it was my favourite and I loved it. I used to hold it in my hand till it was warm and imagine it was the heat from my hand releasing the gold from under the green. Sara's eyes were like that; deep and green as the sea when you are under it, staring up at the sun.

Cold separated my face and neck from the rest of my body. When I opened my eyes I saw Sara. She was lying on her back and I could see the millions of tiny white hairs on her ear. Under the duvet my body was sticky from the heat of being pressed up against hers. My hand was resting on her abdomen and through the layers of her clothing I could feel her stomach going up and down as she breathed. I didn't move for fear of waking her; I just wanted to lie beside her and look at her.

8

Each morning that week I waited, hidden by a wall, just up from their house till I saw Glenn scoot out of their gateway on his bike and head for school. Then I knocked for Sara, leaving it till the last minute so we were almost late and had to hurry, so there was no time to talk.

All week I did this, and at lunchtimes I persuaded her to come to the baker's in the High Street rather than going back to her house, and after school we went to the sweet shop and I bought us both chocolate, then we sat in the rec and ate it, and then sat a little longer, having a smoke. And so I avoided Glenn, and kept Sara to myself. All week, until Friday when Glenn caught up with us just outside the school gates at lunchtime.

'Come back to the house,' he said.

And Sara said yes, and so I said yes, because what else could I say?

'I haven't seen you all week,' he said to me, and the three of us walked together. He put his arm around my shoulders, heavy as a dead man's.

I couldn't put it off forever, I knew I couldn't. I couldn't put *him* off. I couldn't risk losing Sara. So I walked between the two of them, my feet in time with Sara's, my body attached to Glenn's. His arm was a heavy weight, unnatural across my back.

I was on a path now, and I couldn't turn back.

'My mum's out all night tonight.'

Sara squinted into the mirror with one eye as she drew black kohl over the lid of the other. I sat on her bed and watched her. 'And Mark and Rachel have gone to the cinema, though her step-dad thinks she's here of course. So . . .' she threw the eyeliner down among the rest of the clutter and rummaged for lipstick '. . . it's just us four tonight.'

She looked back in the mirror, caught my eye in the reflection and grinned at me. Automatically I grinned back, but I could sense things running out of control now, like I was some kind of puppet, being dangled from strings.

Later, I sat on Glenn's lap again and let him kiss my mouth, my neck, my chest inside the opening of my top. His hair spiked my face so I had to close one eye and watch Sara through the other. Glenn worked his hand up the inside of my thigh and then pressed me through my jeans. It hurt, but he groaned as if it was great. He undid the button and tugged down the zip then scratched and pulled at my knickers.

I let him do all these things because through my one

eye I could see that that was what Sara was letting Andy do to her.

I heard Andy whisper to Sara and she said something back, but I couldn't make out what it was because of the noise Glenn was making kissing my ear. Then Sara quickly put her clothes back where they should be and they stood up.

'We're going to bed,' she said and smirked at me. 'See you in the morning.'

I hated her for a moment, then. It rocked through me like a bolt. I hated her on and off for quite some time after that, though I never let it show. I couldn't let it show, or that would be the end of us. And anyway, to feel hate you have to feel love first, don't you? And I did. I think I felt them both so strongly that they became mixed up and I couldn't tell one from the other.

She was testing me, I was sure of that. Testing me, to see what I would do. To see if I was up to this, if I had what it took. To see if I'd run off home or if I'd still be there in the morning.

I like to think it was loyalty she was after from me.

Glenn smiled at me a slow, half-sleepy smile and I wondered if they'd planned it. I didn't smile back; I couldn't. He sat there a little longer with me rigid on his lap, body screaming to run but unable to, like a cat caught in the headlights. He stroked his fingers up and down on my breast bone, just below my throat. I think this was supposed to be a caress, you know, to relax me a bit. His hand brushed along my open shirt as he did this; I listened to the sound the material made against his skin and I listened to the hiss of the gas fire. I concentrated on these things; I concentrated on sounds. Then his hand went down further as I knew it would, squeezing at my breasts. He shifted himself in the chair then, pressing himself against my leg, deliberately, making sure that I knew what he'd got down there. He rubbed himself against me. He took my hand and put it down on his lap, holding it there for a minute. And then he stood up, pulling me up with him.

Glenn led me upstairs, still holding my hand. I could hear mumbled voices through the closed door to Sara's room, and from time to time they laughed. I thought they might be laughing at me, and I really hated her then. I hated her for setting me up like this. But most of all I hated her for being in there, with Andy, with the door closed, shutting me out.

I held on to that hate while I lay on Glenn's lumpy, unmade bed while he did his horrible best to make love to me. He fumbled with the clasp of my bra and yanked hard at my jeans so that the denim scraped the sides of my thighs. I didn't make it any easier; I didn't know how to. Cold air shivered over my body when he sat back off of me to undo the buttons of his own shirt and pull down his jeans. I kept my head turned to the window, above the bed. The curtains were patterned blue-and-orange and were too small for the window; I fixed my eyes on the black gap between them. I know that girls are all supposed to wonder about their first time and imagine how it might be – but I hadn't. I hadn't thought about it at all.

He came down on top of me with his elbows either side of my arms and his head tipped down between my neck and my shoulder, and he grunted as he tried to push himself into me. When that didn't work he moved so he could get one hand down there and tried to push it in with that. It didn't want to go. He leant up on his elbow and clenched hard on my shoulder like it was a lever; for a moment that hurt more than what his other hand was doing and I tried to press myself into the bed to get away from him, but then he gave one more heave and flopped, panting, down on top of me.

His weight was crushing me; I couldn't move. He had his face buried in the pillow beside me and I heard his breathing gradually slow. He shifted then, and leant over the bed. I thought my ribs would break under him but then he pulled himself off completely, to reach for the box of tissues beside the bed. First I felt the cold and then the wetness; I thought I must be bleeding to death and pressed my thighs together in panic.

'Here.' Glenn took tissues for himself and handed me the rest. I was so ashamed and embarrassed that I wanted to die, but at least he had the grace to turn away. I realised then that it wasn't blood, just *wet*.

He brushed the tissues off the bed on to the floor. A memory flashed up on my mind of something Sara said once, pointing to Glenn's room as we came out of hers. *Urgh, you don't want to go in there*, she'd said. *Tissues all over the floor. Caught him at it the other day.* I'd wondered what she meant. She knew all about boys, sex, but what did I know? Nothing. I bet *she* wasn't lying cold and mortified like the worse thing in the world had just happened to her.

Glenn pulled the blankets up over us and wriggled his arm under my shoulder to pull me to him. The bone in his arm pressed against the nobble at the top of my spine and I didn't know which way to let my head fall. Fat tears spilt and rolled sideways into my ears. 'Ssh . . . it's OK,' Glenn whispered, and wiped away the tears with his free hand. And he kissed the side of my face; little, gentle kisses, and his kindness now after what he'd just done made it worse and I started crying properly.

'Don't cry,' he said. 'I didn't mean to hurt you. I didn't want to hurt you.' He held me close to him and I could hear the thud of his heart and the vibration of his voice through his chest. 'I'd never hurt you, Kate . . .' He spoke softly to me and stroked my hair and my shoulder over and over until his words faded and his hand stilled, and I realized he'd fallen asleep. Then I lay staring into the dark, in Glenn's room instead of Sara's, warm from his body, when all I wanted was to be near to hers.

At some point in the night I heard the door to Sara's room open and every nerve in my body jolted. I was about to dash out of bed, out of the room, when I heard Andy mutter 'Shit' and heavy footfalls on the stairs. I fell back against the pillows, waiting for the pounding of my heart to subside. Glenn hadn't stirred. He hardly stirred all night. Sara fidgeted and snored and made a funny little clicking noise in the back of her throat. Glenn was silent and still as a dead man.

I did sleep, though I thought I never would. I awoke before Glenn. He was lying on his back with the arm that had been around me bent upwards on the pillow. I'd slithered down the bed into the warmth and now as I moved my skin peeled away from his, naked.

I looked around and tried not to think. The room stank of socks and stale cigarette ends, and it was a mess, a horrible mess. Clothes were strewn all over the floor; sweatshirts and tops all twisted up and with their sleeves half inside-out still. My clothes lay tangled on top of his. As I began to climb out to reach them Glenn rolled over and caught me with his arm.

'Where are you going?'

'I've got to get home,' I said, embarrassed at my nakedness. 'I said I'd be back by half-ten.'

He groaned and closed sleepy eyes again. 'Are you coming back later?'

'No. I can't.' I picked up my shirt, and held it in front of me, covering myself up.

'When will I see you then?'

'Well . . . tomorrow . . . I'll see you tomorrow . . .'

He fell back down on the pillow and seemed to be asleep again. I got dressed as fast as I could because of the cold, wishing that I could get my bag from Sara's room. My hairbrush was in it, my toothbrush – everything. I couldn't go home without it. I was pulling my fingers through my hair to try and comb it, and wondering what I should do, when I heard Sara's door open. I stopped, rigid.

Someone whacked on the door, and Sara called, 'Get up you lazy sods.' I heard her run down the stairs and I stuck on my shoes and followed her.

I had to act like I was fine, of course.

She was in the kitchen, filling up the kettle and getting cups out for tea. I stood in the doorway and watched her. She had thick socks on her feet and a huge man's jumper that came down to her thighs, and nothing else. Goosepimples stood out on her bluey-white legs and she jiggled from one foot to the other to fight the cold.

I had to pretend this was all right. This was *normal* for Sara. After all, she had been 'seeing' Andy for some time, and before that she was 'seeing' Mark.

As soon as she'd lit the gas under the kettle Sara said, 'Dying for a pee,' and pushed past me out of the kitchen.

While she was in the loo I went into the bathroom next to it to wash my face and hands. It took ages for the water to run warm. I heard Sara cranking the loo handle to flush it then she came and stood next to me at the sink. I plopped the soap from my hands into hers. She had big hands for a girl, with big knuckles, like Glenn's.

'I've got to have a bath before Glenn gets up,' Sara said as she pulled a towel down from the rail over the bath. 'Don't want him to get all the hot water.'

'I've got to go soon,' I said.

She held the towel and I dried my hands on it. I wished then that there was just us, no Glenn, no Andy, no anybody else but just us. I wished there was no school, no parents, no separate houses, no money getting in the way. I wished that there had been nothing to prove.

'You're going to wear this towel out if you're not careful,' she said.

I stopped rubbing my hands but couldn't look up. Her hands were inches from mine. Across the grey of the towel hers were pink, and mine almost brown, desperate, clinging on.

* * *

I thought I'd look different somehow. I was terrified my parents would be able to tell, that they'd notice some change in me, so I covered my tracks to keep the suspicion down. I made sure I was extra good at home – got on with my homework, that sort of thing.

Everyone at school must have known, but I tried not to hear what they were saying. It seemed they were talking about somebody else, not me. I *felt* like I was somebody else every time Glenn put his arm around me, right there, in the playground. It was obvious we were seeing each other. And Glenn wasn't the sort of boy who'd go out with you and be content holding your hand; everyone knew that.

But it all felt so weird.

I was doing it for Sara, that's what I kept telling myself. It was like they came as a pair, and if I rejected him I'd be rejecting her. I had no choice. I was doing it for Sara.

That is the logic that steered me on. And if it all felt so wrong, I just blanked it out.

9

For Christmas Sara gave me a tiny silver bracelet, so fragile and thin I was afraid to touch it much, and a clasp so stiff and insecure I knew I'd lose it straight away if ever I wore it. We broke up for Christmas at midday and I unwrapped it just outside the school gates; we stood for ages while she did it up for me on my wrist, her fingers struggling with the lock.

'It's gorgeous,' I said, and she looked really pleased.

My present to her was a five-year lockable diary. 'For you to fill with your darkest secrets,' I said, but I wanted her to fill it with me.

I tucked my hand and the bracelet carefully into my glove and we walked through the rec, sharing a fag, passing it between my black woolly fingers and her blue-pink naked ones. It would be days till we saw each other again.

'Happy Crimbo,' I said when we parted.

'Happy Crimbo.'

I stuffed my gloved hands into my pockets and as I did so I felt the bracelet snap and trickle like a cold worm into the palm of my hand.

* * *

I loved Christmas, and the days just before were best of all. All the excitement, the anticipation. Mum never worked over Christmas; it had been a joke between us for years that she always broke up the same day I did, and we did everything together, all the preparation. I'd spend more time with her in the few days before Christmas than I did in the whole rest of the year put together.

We had all these little traditions, unique to us. I thought all families were like that, with their own little ways. I made rum truffles and meringues in the kitchen, and melted chocolate in a bowl over a saucepan to dip orange peel into. I'd done this every year for as long as I could remember. We didn't have crackers in our house, we wrapped sugared almonds in cellophane and ribbons for the table instead. We did this in the living room, spread out on the floor next to the Christmas tree, with the television on showing old Christmassy films. And we made decorations for the table too, poking holly sprigs into that green foamy stuff that gets stuck under your fingernails when you pick at it.

I'd always helped with the food shopping too, queuing up with Mum at the butcher's in the High Street to get the turkey and the ham and loading them into the boot of the car like farcical corpses, then going to the greengrocer's – the one where Sara worked now on Saturdays – and filling our baskets with potatoes and brussels and apples and satsumas. I always got the satsumas, knowing the scent of their skin would stay on my hands; the scent of Christmas.

Two days into the holiday Glenn phoned me at home. He called in the morning at about elevenish and luckily I answered the phone. My mum was upstairs, sorting out presents to take to the cousins. Panic rushed in my head when I heard his voice. He said he had a present for me – he wanted to come round, to see me on my own; but I said no, no, I'd have to meet him somewhere. God, if my parents had any idea I was seeing him they'd go mad, they'd never let me stay at Sara's again.

I didn't have time to go out and get Glenn a present, so I wrapped up a CD that I'd bought for myself a couple of weeks before, even though I knew he had nothing to play it on. I told my mum I needed to do some last minute shopping and met him the next day at three o'clock, outside the estate agent's at the end of the High Street.

He was already there when I arrived, and probably had been for a while because the cold had made his cheeks pink and he was rocking from one foot to the other to keep warm. It felt weird meeting him like that; and I really just wanted to go back to his house and see Sara. But Glenn had other plans. We walked for a bit, away from the shops and through the park, towards the river. I couldn't think of anything to say to him; I hadn't actually been on my own with him before, apart from in his bed.

There were some benches by the river, all pretty damp, but we sat on one anyway. He put his arm around my shoulders, holding me close to him. He'd got me a little gift set of different bath oils and wrapped it up in paper covered in dancing snowmen, and I gave him that CD, feeling a little guilty now.

There was no one around. It was the day before Christmas Eve, when I should have been at the greengrocer's with my mother, picking out the satsumas. It was cold and damp and already starting to get dark; I thought of the shops in the High Street and how brightly lit and busy they would be. Down there by the river we were totally alone.

'Where's Sara?' I asked. 'What's she doing?'

'Forget Sara for five minutes will you?' Glenn said and he suddenly turned and started kissing me, leaning right over me, kiss after kiss. His tongue felt enormous, filling my mouth, pushing into me. My mouth was stretched wide; I couldn't breathe, couldn't swallow, couldn't move.

After a while he pulled away from me a little and stroked my face with his hand; touching my cheek, my lips, pushing back my hair. I could feel myself sliding further and further out of depth.

'I love you,' Glenn said and he had the tightest look in his eyes, sad and happy and gone too far for me to ever turn back from this.

I know he was waiting for me to say it back but I couldn't. The green of his eyes seemed lighter, brighter in the half-dark, and he looked to me hurt already, because that's all he would be, that's all I would be too – and I tried to speak but my throat clogged and no words would come, only tears suddenly, and he stroked me again and said 'Ssh' and then kissed me again, and I clung to him, kissing him back, trying to find feelings where there were none. I *did* love him. I told myself this again and again. I did love him; I *had* to love him.

Now his hands were inside my jacket, under my jumper, up my short denim skirt and between my legs, pressing me through the thick wool of my tights. He pulled back again, and this time he said, 'Good job you've got a skirt on.' Then he half-lifted me off the bench so that he could pull my tights down and I helped him, letting my shoe fall off and wriggling one leg free. He tried to lay me back on the bench but it didn't really work so we ended up on the concrete in front of the bench with my jacket underneath my back and the stones scratching at our bare legs. He pulled my knickers down, getting them off over one foot and leaving them tangled with my woolly tights around the other leg. The cold whooshed at me, at all my warm places, then he was on top of me, the weight of him pressing my legs and bottom into the cold gritty ground till he came, then the cold again and the wet, mixing with the dirt as it ran out of me.

I thought it would get better, after the first time, but I never got used to it, to that thing shoving in at me. I kept telling myself he was Sara's brother, part of her, of the same flesh. I buried my face in his hair, imagining it was her hair. Every time he pushed himself into me I hated it, but I would never give him up. How could I? He was Sara's brother.

I phoned Sara on Christmas morning to wish her Happy Christmas. I phoned between the present-opening and the lunch preparation. There was always a lull in our house then, before Dad returned from picking up my gran and the present-opening started all over again.

It was ages before anyone answered the phone, then Sara said 'Hello' down the line loud, quick, as if she'd been rushing.

'Hello,' I said. 'Happy Christmas.'

'Happy Christmas,' she said back, automatically. She sounded surprised to hear from me.

'What were you doing?' I asked.

'I was in the kitchen. Getting the potatoes on.' There

was a slight question in her voice; I got the feeling she was wondering why I'd rung.

'Oh, right,' I said, feeling a little awkward now because she wasn't exactly chatty. 'Are you having a nice time?'

'All right,' she answered, but she didn't ask me. There was silence down the line for a moment, then she said, 'Look, I'd better go. I've got the water boiling.'

She hung up before me and I stood there, listening to the line buzzing for a second. I'd phoned her up full of Christmas cheer and now that cheer had gone. I imagined that Christmas Day at Sara's house was very different to Christmas Day at mine.

There was just the three of us on Christmas Day, and my grandmother, but on Boxing Day we piled into the car with loads more presents and drove to my Aunty Fran's house in Caversham. They had a fairly big house but it never felt big on Boxing Day with my aunt and uncle, the three boy cousins and my other gran and grandpa all crowded into the living room, with the boys' toys everywhere and their two dogs bounding around all the time.

My Aunty Fran always did a buffet for lunch and my mum would bring something along too, a couple of salads or something, and I'd just eat those because I never much fancied the other stuff with those dogs yapping at the table, drooling at the food. One year I'd had a bowl of Aunty Fran's trifle and there'd been a dog hair, right there in the custard.

'Not eating much, Kate?' my aunt would always say and there'd be the usual comparison between my bird-like appetite and those of her growing boys. She'd try and pile up my plate, and though I didn't really want to eat anything I still loved the fuss she made over me. They had the same dark colouring, her and my mum, but apart from that you'd never know they were sisters.

After lunch I'd have to go upstairs with Ben, the oldest of the boys, and look at his CD collection and talk about school. He was all right, Ben, but really shy and it was hard work making conversation with someone you only saw once or twice a year. And this year he'd broken out in spots, great whoppers, all over his chin and nose, making him more self-conscious than ever. The other two, Tom and James, would inevitably follow us upstairs and start jumping on Ben's bed and clambering all over me. They were dead cute really, if a little annoying. And at least upstairs we were away from those dogs.

Then on the way home, as soon as we were out of sight and could stop waving, my dad would say, 'Well that's that over for another year.'

And my mum would agree with him, making some

comment like, 'I know she's my sister but her hygiene standards leave something to be desired. Did you *see* the kitchen? And those dogs, everywhere?'

I know she had a point and everything but even so I felt this creeping anger on my aunty's behalf. I mean, how could they go along, pretend to enjoy it, then bitch about it on the way home? They did this every year and I felt sorry for my poor aunty. She was always so pleased to see us.

And anyway, dogs or no dogs, I loved it at my cousins' house. At least it wasn't *quiet* all the time.

On the day after Boxing Day I went round Sara's. Her mother was there this time. I'd never met her before. I know that sounds incredible; I spent so much time at their house that you'd think I must have met her by now, lots of times. But I hadn't. She seemed to spend every day at the shop, even weekends. Sara said she was having a really hard time, trying to keep the business going all by herself, and that her dad was being a total git over the divorce and the money and everything. On the Saturday nights that I stayed over at Sara's her mum would always be out and if she came back before we went to bed I'd stay in the living room, out of the way, while Sara or Glenn or both of them went out to deal with her. I'd heard her talking to them. I'd heard her swearing and I'd heard her crying, but I'd never met her.

And in the mornings I'd be long gone before she was awake.

She was in the kitchen when I got there, rummaging through piles of cutting books and invoices at the table, shoving papers into a bag and saying to Sara, 'You know I have to go in. I have no choice.'

Sara was drying up dishes, putting away pans, slamming things around and insisting, 'Well, I'll cook tonight, shall I? You will be home for tea, won't you?'

She had dark hair, Sara's mother, which struck me as odd but I supposed Sara and Glenn must take after their dad instead. Her hair was cut short and layered and streaked with grey all down one side, spreading back from her forehead. She was wearing a black straight skirt that was a bit too tight and rolled up a little round the middle, and a cream shirt that was tucked in at the front but had started to come out a bit at the back as she moved. When the bag was full she put it down by the back door, next to the two that were already there. Plastic carrier bags, stuffed with papers and files, tearing in places where hard corners of cardboard poked through. I'd climbed over them when I came in. The bags sagged over a little and Sara's mother straightened them up with her foot. She had black sling-back shoes on her feet and black tights; on the back of her foot just above her heel the nylon of her tights had stretched and thinned into a pyramid shape; they would be laddered within the hour.

I stood in the kitchen, trying to keep out of the way while she sorted out her things, thinking she might mind that I was there all the time, seeing all their lives, but she barely glanced at me, just said, 'Hello, love, had a nice Christmas?' as she stooped to gather up her bags. She had a tired face and very tired eyes, not green like Sara's but grey. And faded, like there'd been some colour there once but most of it had drained away, over time.

They'd stuck a little silver tinsel tree on top of a box, next to the TV, and hung baubles on it.

We sat on the sofa, the three of us, with me sitting sideways on Glenn's lap with my legs up and my feet tucked under Sara's bum, and watched Christmas TV. And we ate Quality Street from the huge tin they had, and drank whiskey in little swigs straight from the bottle. For three days in a row we did this, till the chocolates were all gone.

And on the third day I stayed over lunchtime, and Rachel came round too, and Sara cooked chips for us all in a dented pan on the stove. 'Real chips,' Rachel said. 'You just wait till you try them.'

I peeled the potatoes over the sink, using a knife so blunt that it cut away hunks of potato as well as skin, and Rachel chopped them at the table. There were tons of potatoes; on the Saturday before Christmas the greengrocer had let Sara take home extra, for free. Sara took a Pyrex bowl of hard fat out of the fridge, scooped a lump out with a spoon and threw it into the pan to heat. She'd got the heat up too high and the fat started sizzling, and when she threw in the potatoes it roared and popped. Fat-smoke filled the kitchen and the hall and the whole house, and we had to open up all the windows to try and clear the air. It stings your eyes, fat-smoke.

She could only do a few chips at a time because the pan was small, and it was a precarious skill, keeping the fat from actually catching fire. Every so often the pan would start crackling dangerously and she'd have to lift it right off the stove, holding it as far away from her body as possible with her arm stretched out so the fat didn't spit at her. Then when it quietened down again she'd carry on, lifting each batch out of the pan with an old wire sieve, holding it there to drain for a minute before quickly turning to the table and dumping the chips straight on to plates. Drops of hot fat flew from the sieve as she turned and the floor around her feet grew slippery. Really she could have done with some kitchen towel to wipe that floor and put on those plates, but there wasn't any.

By the time she'd finished, her hands and her face were red and glistening. She put the pan down on the ground outside the back door to cool and the steam off it thickened and hissed in the cold air. The chips were greasy and soggy and pretty disgusting but we smothered them in salt, and Rachel ran home to get some vinegar and we drowned them in that. It was malt vinegar and it mingled with the grease on the plates, turning it brown.

When the fat in the pan had cooled down enough Sara poured it back into the Pyrex bowl, to use another day. It looked like honey, dark and almost clear on top of the hard yellow-white stuff already in the bowl.

On the Friday of that week Sara came to my house. It was the only time that she ever came to my house in the whole time that I knew her.

I should have known it was a bad idea, but my mum and dad had been going on about the fact that I was always round Sara's and that she'd never been to our house, not even once; they'd never even met her.

'Who is the mysterious Sara?' my Dad kept saying, in that really annoying way that made my toes curl.

And anyway, I wanted to be alone with her for a bit, without Glen, so I asked her and she came.

But the minute I opened the front door to let her in I wanted to slam it again in her sullen face.

I asked her to take her trainers off in the hall, because it's what we all did in our house. 'Got a cream carpet,' I apologized, but she raised her eyebrows at me and sort of half-smirked, as if this was too ridiculous for words. Of course at Sara's house you needed to keep your shoes on, to keep your feet clean. She leant against the wall and took them off one at a time, loosening the laces just a little then using one foot to press down on the heel of the other shoe so that she could pull that foot out. She always took her trainers off like this and the insides at the back were badly worn and broken down. Then she stood up and folded her arms across her chest and she kept them there, like a barrier between us.

She didn't relax for a minute.

Our house was still full of Christmas; my mum and dad were both home, and for lunch Mum put out French bread and cheese and pickles and things in the dining room for us to help ourselves. Sara hardly spoke, to my parents or to me; from the moment she arrived she just had such an *attitude*, call it what you will, I don't know, such *resentment*, that fucking chip on her fucking shoulder that will fuck her up till the end of her days . . .

She looked at my house and she stained it with her eyes. She followed me up the stairs, feet silent behind me, and came like a curse into my bedroom, to be always there, forever more, her memory a dark heavy blot.

Why can we not choose who we love?

I sat on the bed and followed her face in the mirror over my dressing table as she looked around. 'Very nice,' she muttered, like she didn't mean it.

First she went for my CD collection. 'Very nice,' she said again, with such a sneer in her voice. She flipped out my Eminem CD and stuck it in my CD player, turning it up really loud. My parents can't stand Eminem, never mind at that volume.

'Turn it down,' I said, and she looked at me like I was the most suburban thing on earth. Of course we didn't have this problem at her house, because there was no decent CD player, and no parents either, most of the time.

Then she started looking at the things on my dressing table. There wasn't much there, just my jewellery box, the china dish from Portugal with all my bits and bobs in, and my hair brush and things like that. I watched her face in the mirror as she picked up each thing in turn and put it down again in its place. I wondered if she was thinking of her own stuff, the broken make-up compacts and cosmetic bottles with the lids left off, those same lids lost among the empty cigarette packets and match boxes and lipsticks and hair clips and all the other junk heaped on top of her own chest of drawers. I wondered if she was *comparing*.

Of course she was. I could see it in her face.

'Let's see what you've got in here, then,' she said next and opened the wardrobe.

I had shelves all down one side of my wardrobe, crammed with jumpers, T-shirts, jeans and things, all neatly folded. Sara looked for something to pick on and she found it, on the bottom shelf. My old ballet shoes and my leotard, left there from years and years ago.

'Oh, *what?*' she shrieked. 'Check this out!' And she pulled them out, holding them up and then falling back on to my bed, laughing like she was going to die, like they were just too hilarious for words. Which of course they weren't. They were just my old ballet things.

She poked around all my things till I couldn't stand it any more, couldn't stand the sneer on her face and the vibes, all those dark, dark vibes fizzing out of her, so we went out then, just for a walk around the houses and a smoke, until it was time for her to go.

I wished she'd never come. I wished it because I knew from the look on her face that she wished it too.

'Your house is nice,' she said, just as we were parting, at the end of my road. She said it slyly, like an accusation, watching for my reaction.

I didn't react. I felt her judging me as I must not judge her and I minded, I felt angry and I felt some shift from the way things had been, but I didn't react. I knew better than to do that.

When Sara'd gone home I sat in my room and took the bracelet she'd given me out from my jewellery box and draped it over my wrist. I couldn't do it up because of the broken clasp, so I just held out my hand and balanced it there. The bracelet was so incredibly tiny and delicate. I tried to imagine her choosing it. I imagined what she might have been thinking, what she might have been feeling, about me. It was so special, made even more so because Sara had so little money, yet she'd got this for me.

For a second I wondered if she did pay for it at all. But when did I become so cynical? The thought would have been there just the same, however she'd got it. She'd been thinking about me, that was what mattered.

Jewellery is so special, isn't it? It's what lovers give. Oh I don't mean earrings and pendants, but chains, to go round your neck or your wrist. Chains.

Suddenly I felt so sad that the bracelet was broken. The clasp had snapped right off, away from the chain; I couldn't possibly fix it. It seemed symbolic, right then. I started to cry; I *let* myself cry. It eased the pressure inside a little. I sat in my room and wallowed in my heartache, pining.

Later, I heard Mum and Dad talking about us, about Sara and me. I'd been up in my room for ages and was about to come downstairs; I opened the door then stopped still, listening.

They were down in the kitchen but I could hear them from there. I knew it was serious. No one ever raised their voices in our house.

'. . . I know, Gina, but we have to handle this carefully.'
My dad's voice was loud but slow, like he was working so
hard to hold on to his patience. I hated it when he spoke
in that way, as if everyone apart him was stupid.

'Oh for goodness' sake!' My mother hated it too; *she*
just sounded petulant.

'Gina love—'

'You saw her, Tony,' my mother broke in, and I held
my breath, not wanting to move. They were talking
about *Sara*.

'I know, and I agree but—'

'Is that the sort of friend you want for Kate?'

'No, it isn't—' my dad started but my mum cut right
across him.

'If we'd sent her to St Mary's this wouldn't have
happened,' she snapped.

I opened the door a little wider and crept out on to
the landing, heart thumping; *crept* so that the
floorboards didn't creak. I wanted to hear everything.

'We don't know that,' my dad replied. 'And there's
no point in going over it now.' My mum snorted and he
went on, 'It was your choice as well as mine.' She
snorted again and he said, 'Yes it was, Gina. It was.'

I don't know which I hated most, my dad's terminal
hypocrisy or my mum's out-and-out snobbery. They were
as bad as each other, poking themselves up. I listened,
with the rage hissing up inside my head. Who were they

to talk about me and choices in the same breath? What am I? Some sort of *experiment*?

'And do you want *our daughter* going around looking like a common tart?' my mum carried on and her voice was like ice.

Bitch, I thought. *Is that what you think?*

'Of course I don't—'

'Because she does, you know. All that black make-up around her eyes. Or hadn't you noticed?'

'Of course I've noticed. And I don't like it any more than you do.'

My mum mumbled something I couldn't hear and he went on, 'What do you want me to do? Ban her from seeing her?'

'Oh don't be ridiculous,' she snapped now.

'Look, she's just going through a phase,' my dad said and his voice was tight. This was as close as they ever came to arguing. 'Rein in too hard and she'll buck away.'

'Oh honestly, Tony, don't be so bloody liberal.'

'Leave it, Gina,' my dad said. 'It's just a phase. She'll grow out of it.'

But obviously she didn't leave it, because on the Sunday evening before school went back Dad knocked on the door to my room and came in and said he'd like a little chat. I was sitting on my bed, sorting my books out for Monday.

'Your mother and I have been talking,' he said, 'and we feel that perhaps you should start seeing more of your other friends.' He sat on the end of my bed and I just ignored him.

'Juliet and Ruth, for instance,' he said. He wiped his hands up and down his thighs, then clapped them together, all falsely jolly, and clasped them on his knees. 'Why not have them round here on Saturday night? Have a bit of a get-together. You haven't had your friends round here much lately—'

'They are not my friends.' I didn't even look at him; I was still smarting at the way they had talked about me, at his idea that I was going through a *phase*, or that I was some creature, to be reined in. I carried on getting my things together and shoving them into my bag.

'And Sara too of course, but . . .' He sighed, and I stopped what I was doing and waited for him to get to the point. 'Kate,' he said eventually, 'it isn't healthy to spend so much time with one person.' His choice of words really caught me. *He knows*, I thought, *he knows that I love her.*

I stared at him and the heat rushed over my body, up into my face.

'You need lots of friends.' He shook his head, waved his hand in impatience. 'I don't want you being too *influenced* by any one person.'

What kind of word was that? *Influenced?* What was I,

some half-wit, that I couldn't think for myself? Now it was anger, hot in my face, thick on my tongue. 'You don't like her.' My dad flinched slightly at this simple, simple truth – but that wasn't enough for me; I wanted to see him really squirm. '*Why* don't you like her?'

I wanted him to spell it out, to say what he was really thinking and choke on all his hypocritical ideals, but he didn't of course. He'd die rather than admit to being a snob. Instead he said, 'It isn't that, Kate. It's not that we don't *like* her. But you've changed. We are concerned about you.'

'Sara's my best friend. You can't stop me being friends with her.' I could hear my voice rising, becoming hysterical. Dad heard it too, and his face started to redden. He spread his hands out towards me, struggling for words. As if he expected me to make this *easier* for him.

'No of course not,' he said at last, really quite flustered now. 'But see your other friends too—'

'Ruth and Juliet are not my friends!' I shouted, facing him now. *Daring* him.

I glared at him, he stared at me. I think we were both surprised by my anger.

'Sara's my friend,' I said. 'You can't change that.'

The phrases *This is not the end of the matter* and *We will discuss this more later* come to mind, but I don't know if he said them then or later, or if it's just my memory throwing them in for the ride. Certainly there was an air of such words around the house that evening, the next day, and on and off for all of the days of all of the months that followed.

It all reminded me of something else, from years before; another occasion when my parents had deemed it necessary for us to have a little chat. Back in the last year of infant school I made friends with a girl called Shannon Harding. This would have been the one year when Juliet and I were in separate classes.

Shannon had two brothers and a sister, all younger than her, and her dad worked at the tip, sorting out the rubbish. She told me he often brought things home with him on the back of his van. She made it sound really exciting, like treasure. My dad never brought anything home from work.

I went back to Shannon's house one day after school – for tea, I thought. She lived in one of the council houses at the back of the school. Her mum met us at the school gates with one of the little brothers and the sister sitting on top of each other in an old fold-up pushchair – one of those ones with a striped, nylon strip to sit in, like a deck chair – and the other brother balanced on the back, standing on the bit of frame that crossed from one wheel to the other. The wheels of the pushchair were bending outwards under all this weight and the whole thing looked like it would collapse at any moment. Shannon's mum was quite small and thin and she had to lean right forward over this pushchair, bracing all her weight behind the load, to get it moving. We walked down the alley into the council estate, Shannon and me skipping ahead, careful not to tread in the dog mess.

They had a bed in their front garden. A big old-fashioned one with a pink headboard, and a squashy old mattress with a great hole picked in the middle so the fluff and the springs were coming out. Shannon said the birds and the mice had made the hole, trying to make their nests. It was a hot day; Shannon's mum took the little ones inside but we stayed out the front, playing. There was a lot of stuff in the front garden, as well as the bed. There was an old pram that we took it in turns to squeeze ourselves into, and a bike with only one wheel, and various planks of wood that we stacked against the bed to make a den.

I still remember the look on my dad's face when he came to pick me up at six o'clock. He stood on their pathway with the sun in his eyes, squinting at me. He'd come straight from work but he'd taken his jacket off and loosened his tie because of the heat. Something else I remember about that day is that I'd had a nosebleed at school – I had loads of nosebleeds, when I was little – and the blood had dripped and dried in brown splodges all down the front of my green school dress. I must have looked quite at home in Shannon's garden with my dress all stained and my hands and knees grubby from clambering in and out of our den, in the dirt.

'Come on, Kate,' he said. 'It's time to go.'

We didn't knock on the door to say goodbye to Shannon's mum. There didn't seem much point as I hadn't seen her since we got home. We hadn't been in the house at all, not even to go to the loo. Shannon had weed in the garden behind our den when we'd built it, and later, when I'd been bursting, I'd done the same, crouching down in the long grass.

We left Shannon in the front garden, bouncing up and down on the bed. She bounced high, oblivious to my dad's lack of manners as he took my hand and marched me to his car.

My dad asked me two things on the way home. He said did Shannon's mother walk me back from school, and did she know we were playing out the front? I answered yes to both and he nodded, and said nothing more. He didn't ask me if I'd had a nice time. He didn't even ask what I'd had for tea, which was just as well, as I hadn't had anything.

I went to bed that night hungry and with the unsettling feeling that I'd done something wrong, but not knowing what. And sure enough it came the next day, the little chat about Shannon not being the right sort of friend for me and wouldn't I be much happier with Juliet and the other nice girls that I normally played with. Oh, I know what they meant. What they meant was they didn't want me playing with someone with nits in her hair and a bed in her front garden.

They needn't have bothered with the chat. Soon after that things started disappearing from my pencil case, favourite felt pens and rubbers and things. Other children lost things too and they all turned up in Shannon's desk. I went off Shannon pretty quickly then anyway.

My parents probably thought it was their little chat that had steered me away from Shannon. They didn't know about the stealing. They probably thought the chat had done the job nicely, and I expect they thought it would work just as well now, with Sara.

How wrong can you be? There's nothing like a bit of outside conflict to intensify the determined in love.

I told Sara about it on Monday, when school went back.

'Honestly it's just so unreal,' I moaned. This was lunchtime and we were on our way back to her house, having a smoke on the way. 'They want to control me – have Juliet and Ruth round! I mean, can you imagine? They think they can pick my friends for me . . .'

I took a deep drag on the cigarette and passed it to her. She took it, looked at it and wiped the filter on the sleeve of her denim jacket before sticking it in her mouth. I waited for a response from her. I thought she would *care*, I thought she would say something, I thought she would say a million things – but she didn't so I went on, 'They can't stop me seeing you. What are they going to do – lock me up at the weekend?'

Still Sara didn't say anything, she just kept walking, looking at the ground. I wasn't even sure if she was listening.

'They can't split us up,' I said, and I wanted her to say *No, no, they'll never split us up*. I wanted her to sympathise, say *Poor you* or something. Just *something*. 'They can't rule my life for me . . .'

Now she stopped and looked at me. And she said, 'Then don't let them,' slowly, as if to shut me up, as if she just didn't want to hear any more.

10

Sara and I caught the bus after school one day – it was a Wednesday soon after we'd gone back after Christmas – and we went to Lewiston, shopping. I had some money I'd been given for Christmas and I wanted to buy something to wear, and I wanted her to help me choose it.

I looked forward to it all day. At half-past three we walked down to the end of the road near the school where the bus stopped and stood with all the kids that always took the bus every day, the ones that lived in Lewiston and Eppingham Hill and had to *travel* to get to our school; the worldly ones.

We sat at the back, on our own. All the other kids huddled at the front, most of them standing, and swaying about and deliberately bumping into each other every time the bus slowed to stop or turn round a bend. This was obviously some sort of weird game or ritual. There must have been about fifteen of them, all jostling together in that small space. From the back of the bus Sara and I watched them like they were strange animals.

You weren't allowed to smoke on the bus, but

everyone knows bus drivers don't care so we lit up anyway, sharing one cigarette between us like we always did, cupping it in our hands as we passed it back and forth, keeping it down low, just in case.

It took about twenty minutes, by bus, to Lewiston. We smoked our cigarette, watched the kids at the front, and looked out of the window, as if there was a view. It was important, this journey, to me at least. It was me and Sara, going somewhere.

Stop by stop the weirdos at the front got off till there was just us left, just us going all the way into town. Slunk down at the back, reclining, in our own private bus being driven by our own private driver – just us. When we got off Sara said, 'Cheers, mate,' to the driver, then called him a grumpy bastard because he ignored her.

We went to McDonald's first and I bought us milkshakes, which we carried with us round the shops. There were only three shops in the mall in Lewiston worth looking in: the first was just inside the entrance and OK for jeans and things like that – but I wanted something special; then there was Dorothy Perkins – all right but a bit dull; but the main shop, the one where you had to go, the one where you'd always find something you wanted even though the assistants were total bitches, was It Girl. In Lewiston there was a huge It Girl, right in the middle of the precinct. The whole front of the shop opened up and it was just packed with clothes, rail upon rail, all bright colours, all dead cheap, all gorgeous. Music blared out from the shop, you could hear it the minute you walked through the precinct doors. I always hated going into It Girl on my own. The assistants looked at you as if you were the fattest, ugliest, frumpiest creature ever to insult their presence; you'd touch the clothes and they'd fall off the hangers; you'd ask to try something on and your voice would come out a squeak; you'd trip on the stairs on the way up to the changing room.

Sara was not phased by them. On the contrary, she saw them as a challenge. As soon as we walked in there were hawk eyes upon us, watching us, looking us up and down, looking at our hair, our clothes, our shoes. That's the thing about bitches: they always look at your shoes. From an early, early age, bitches can tell in a glance what shop your shoes came from, and that your mother took you shopping to buy them, had you properly measured and fitted, that you are brainy, you are square, you are not one of them.

The bitch in It Girl glanced over Sara's trainers then took in every millimetre of my black leather shoes with her stare. Sara held her milkshake in one hand and ran the other hand over a rack of shirts, briskly, so they bobbed and swayed and the hangers clanged together. The assistant glared at her.

'How many can we try on?' Sara asked, fingering the clothes.

'Four each,' the assistant sneered and Sara took a last slurp on her milkshake, and burped loudly.

The changing room was up a long flight of stairs, where there was no air and the stench of feet got stronger with every step. It was a communal changing room: one stuffy room right at the top. Sara sat down on the floor with our bags while I tried on clothes under bright, life-stripping lights. I had twenty-five pounds, enough for one thing, but there were two things I really liked, two tops. I tried on one and Sara said, 'That's gorgeous.' I tried on the other and she said, 'Now you've got to get that.'

I dressed again, back into my old clothes, and stood in front of the mirror, holding both tops up in front of me in turn, trying to decide.

'You could have them both you know,' Sara said.

'I've only got twenty-five pounds.'

Sara shrugged, but I knew what she meant.

When we got to the bottom of the stairs I said, 'I think I'll get this one,' hung the others on the rack by the door and went to pay.

She stuffed the other top inside my jacket. She did it so quick I had to let her. I folded my arms to keep it there, flattened against my body. I had no choice; I was terrified it would fall out, and be seen. Then she shoved me towards the open doors and at the exact moment the alarm from the security tag started bleeping she picked off some dress from the rail nearest the exit, waved it about as if looking at it, and when the assistant came over said, 'Oh sorry is that me?', handed the dress to her and then we were both outside the shop, slowly ambling away.

I could not have walked faster anyway, I could not have run. My legs were like a dummy's legs, unwilling to move. My heart was beating so hard it actually hurt. I thought at any moment I would feel a hand on my shoulder, hear some deep voice saying *Just a minute, Miss* and then that woman from the shop would run, pointing at me, shrieking *Yes it was her!*

Everyone seemed to be staring at us.

Sara led us slowly out of the precinct, out on to the main street, taking her time, looking in shop windows, keeping up the chat all the while. It seemed that once we got outside we'd got away with it. Sara pushed me with her elbow and burst out laughing like it was the most hilarious thing, but I did not find it funny at all. Even in the cold air my face was still burning. I was still waiting for that hand on my shoulder, that voice in my ear.

'Sara, how could you?' I hissed at her, wishing she'd stop laughing. People were looking, I knew they were.

'Easy. You saw how easy. It's only a shirt. They won't miss it.' But when I still didn't laugh she changed her tone and said, 'And anyway *I* didn't. *You* did.'

Yes *I* did, and *I* felt guilty forever more.

11

'Saturday Club again, is it?'

He tried to make a joke of it, but my dad's jokes were pretty feeble at the best of times.

'Oh come on, Dad.' I made myself a cup of tea but I didn't offer him one. I wanted him to just go away and leave me alone but he hung around the kitchen, annoying me. I could feel him watching me, wanting to say something and floundering. I stirred my tea, put down the spoon, faced him, and got in first. 'Why don't you trust me?'

'It's not that, Katie, you know it isn't.' He sighed, biting down on the corner of his lip the way he always did when he was agitated, and there was a tiny muscle, like a pulse, flickering in his neck just behind his jaw. 'But why *Sara's* all the time?'

'She is my friend.' I said it slowly, spelling it out like he was stupid, and the colour began to rise across his cheekbones.

'But why is it so important that you stay there all the time?' he persisted. 'What do you get up to round there?'

'We watch DVDs. What do you think we get up to?'

He raised his hand and drew a finger across my cheek, pressed it under my chin and tilted my head back. He tapped at my chin with his finger, searching my eyes, but he would see nothing there, nothing. 'You are still our daughter, Kate. Remember that.' I held his gaze, and eventually he sighed again and lowered his finger. 'OK,' he said. 'You can go to Sara's tonight. But not every week.'

And I just thought *Big deal – I'm going anyway, you just try and stop me.*

This is how it would go: my dad, who did not want me to go there, would drop me off in the car at about seven o'clock. I'd knock on the kitchen door; someone would always be there, Sara, or Sara and Glenn, or Sara and Rachel. Others would soon be coming; others would have gone out for beer. When we were all there, all six of us, we'd move into the living room. We'd sit about in our pairs, we'd play cards, we'd talk and smoke until the air was cloudy and our heads were getting heavy. My dad's phone call at exactly ten o'clock would be like our cue to move on to the next stage. I'd answer the phone, speak to my dad, then come back into the living room. Sometimes someone would have turned the light out, sometimes they wouldn't have bothered. Now Sara and Andy would be on the sofa, snogging; Rachel and Mark would be in one of the chairs. Glenn would be in the other chair, waiting for me; he'd pull me down to him. I'd sit on his lap and we'd start to snog too, kissing and kissing till my chin was wet.

The next cue would come at just before half past ten, when Rachel had to go home. In half an hour they'd have done a lot in that chair, Rachel and Mark, though not everything. It elevated them somehow, that they had not done everything.

Rachel would get up and smooth down her clothes. Mark would go outside with her and stand in the shadow of the tree out the front, watching to see that she got safely into her own house. Then he'd go on home. It was a different love, theirs. It was the sort of love you ought to have, when you are fifteen.

At this point we might sometimes pause for a drink or a cigarette. Someone might even persuade Sara to go out into the cold kitchen to make tea, although this wasn't very likely. And then the snogging would begin again, and if the light wasn't out before then it certainly would be by now.

It was OK when there was still all four of us, in that room. It was OK when Sara was there. The dark and the quiet would wrap themselves around us and I felt like I was just copying her. But then Sara and Andy would unravel themselves from the sofa and go on to the next stage, upstairs.

They'd always go up first. I knew it would come and

I dreaded it. I'd watch Sara get up from the sofa, and go out of the room.

And then I'd be left with her brother.

When I looked at Glenn, I saw Sara. Oh I don't mean that literally, but I looked for pieces of her in him. I saw the differences, like the fact that his hair was little paler than hers and coarser, and his skin a little pinker with a blush to it at times, on his cheekbones when he was hot or cold and on his chest when he was making love to me. Sara's colour never changed; even when she was angry her skin remained alabaster-white, pure, perfect. I saw these differences but I minimalized them. And I concentrated on the similarities; the precious things. He had the same angular features as Sara, the same high, jutting cheekbones that were probably better suited on a boy's face really, and the same eyes, almost. Almost as green.

He didn't smell like her, but sometimes I would catch a trace of her scent on him, on his face for instance, if he'd used the same towel as her, or on his hands, and my chest would ache so much that I felt that I actually was loving both of them. And sometimes, watching him sleep, in the almost-dark of his room I would half-close my eyes and let my vision blurr and then I would see *her* face, super-imposed over his.

* * *

I did love him. I told myself this again and again. I did love him. I must have done.

12

Someone had written *Sara Williams is a slag* on the wall above the sinks, in thick black letters, for everyone to see. I saw it the minute I pushed through the door. Sara saw it too; she had been talking about something, I can't remember what now, but she stopped sharp. For seconds there was just the clatter of our shoes on the tiled floor, slowing, stopping, stopping after our voices did because I suppose the message from our brains must take longer to get all the way down there, to our feet.

Sara stood, frozen. I looked at her, looked at the wall, looked back at her again, at her white, white face, so pale that even her lips were nearly white and her eyes were glittering. I didn't know what she would do. I didn't know what I should do. We stood like that, as if trapped in honey, for long, long seconds.

And then someone snickered, from one of the cubicles. I snapped round and looked at the gaps under the doors.

You can fit five girls easily into one cubicle, it is done all the time at break, five girls, sharing a fag. One stands with her feet slightly apart so that when the duty teacher comes round and glances under the doors, catching smokers, it looks as if there's just one person in there, sitting on the loo. The others stand on the loo seat, holding on to each other for balance, keeping bent down so their heads can't be seen over the top. It is done all the time. I haven't done it. With Sara and me there has only ever been us, no one else to have to squeeze in.

I looked, I saw bags on the floor and shoes. In moments, those shoes changed to other shoes, then disappeared altogether; suddenly I saw a face, down by the floor, trying to peer out and the snickering turned into screeches, howls of laughter and *Oh my Gods* and *For fuck's sakes* . . .

Sara hurled around and was gone, out the door.

She was away, down the corridor, out across the playground. I ran to catch her up. She was storming towards the gates; she didn't slow down. I trotted along beside her, puffing to keep up.

'It wasn't them, you know,' I said, as if that could make any difference, as if that might make it better somehow. 'It can't have been them.' I said this as if I was some kind of detective; I'd got my lead and I wouldn't let go, I couldn't let go. It wasn't them, whoever they were, hiding in the loo. It wasn't them because you wouldn't write that and hang around and risk getting caught. There was other writing on the walls, of course, lots of it, but in little scratchy marks, in biro, in pencil. Whoever wrote *this* really meant it, really wanted it to be seen.

It wasn't them, but what difference did that make? Someone wrote it, the rest would see it. It was there for everyone, from everyone. That's what Sara thought, I know she did.

'I don't care anyway,' Sara said, though clearly she did. There wasn't time to go to her house, and even if there had been she didn't want to go there now anyway because Glenn would be there and if she told him what had happened he'd go mad, he'd kill those bitches in the loos, even if they weren't the ones who had written it.

So we stood in the rec, till the end of lunch break. We had been sitting on our usual bench, just inside the gate but it had started raining. It was raining quite hard now and we were standing, sheltering, under the porch of the Scout hut. The rain pattered noisily down on the roof above our heads and we were both shivering from the cold.

'None of this matters,' Sara said, teeth chattering over the words. 'All these bastards –' she gestured with her hand, gestured to the world '– don't mean a thing. Not a thing. None of them.'

'Oh thanks,' I said, breath fogging into the cold, damp air. 'And what about me? Do I mean anything?'

She shrugged her shoulders. We'd both got pretty wet

in the rain and Sara's ears were scarlet, raw from the cold where they showed through the strands of her hair. 'Ask me that in ten years' time,' she said. 'If you're still around. If I'm still around. In ten years' time this will all be gone. I will be gone. None of it matters.' She took a last long drag on her fag and flicked the butt out into the rain. 'Glenn matters. Rachel matters, and my mum. The rest can just go to hell.'

Including me, I suppose she meant.

We started going in the other loos after that, the ones on the top floor of the new block, by the music room. Nobody much went in those loos except the swots that did music, so we had the place pretty much to ourselves. We started meeting up there between lessons, and at break time if it was raining and we didn't want to go outside. The teachers never bothered checking in there so we could smoke by the sinks instead of having to hide in a cubicle, and if one of the swots came in we'd just stick our cigarettes behind our backs, out of sight, just *in case* one of them split on us.

There were big windows over the sinks that opened just enough for you to get your head out if you climbed up on to the basins. I didn't climb up but Sara did, while I kept watch at the door. When she saw someone walking below, someone she didn't like, she'd say, 'Watch out, sweetheart,' and flick her cigarette butt, still burning, down at them, or worse than this, she'd fill her mouth up with spit and let it fall out, thick, slow, timing it to land on their heads.

And so she took her revenge, on anyone who she thought might have ever written, spoken or thought a bad thing about her – and that must have added up to just about half the school.

I don't know if Sara ever went in the main loos again. Maybe she didn't. Maybe she never saw what else got written there, but I did. The first time was only about a week or so after the graffiti incident, after we'd started going up to the new block instead. I'd just come out of Maths on the ground floor and I was dying for a pee so I quickly dashed into the main loos, on my way to French. There were quite a few girls in there; there always were, banging doors, going in and out. Not like upstairs.

When I washed my hands I saw that underneath *Sara Williams is a slag* someone had written *So is Kate Harper*, and beside this, scratched in red biro, someone else had added *Hear, hear.*

I didn't think to cross it out, then. I wouldn't have had the nerve to anyway, with other people around. So I quickly washed my hands with the heat burning in my face, and got out, pretending that I hadn't seen it, wishing that I hadn't.

155

It was weeks before I went in there again, and then it was only because I had to, and by then things were very different anyway.

It didn't matter what anyone else thought. I would rather have just one Sara than a million other friends. Sara was all that mattered. I could not care about anyone else. We had ourselves, we had each other.

And we had our own little group. The six of us, when we were together, we were more than friends. We were a *family*. We didn't need anyone else.

I had this sort of *dream*, I think I can call it that. I dreamt that as soon as I was old enough I'd sort of *marry* Glenn and move in with them, into their house. Sara's mother was so elusive through all this time that in my dream I easily swiped her out entirely. In my dream there was just us, Glenn and me and Sara, the three of us together, living in that house. If I really let myself go I imagined it happening sooner, while we were still at school. I sent my parents and my own home and everything in it away, off into oblivion, and had myself there, at number 17, Kidderminster Avenue, with my few precious things beside the spare bed in Sara's room, *my* bed. And there I lived, my world reduced to a corner of her bedroom, and from there I came and went, and so we lived, the three of us, in that house, looking after ourselves, like babes in Toyland. In my dream, I'd open the door to the others on a Saturday night and in they'd come, Andy, Mark, Rachel, and things would go as they always did because I couldn't think of a substitute for that, but for all the minutes of all the days in between there'd be just us. Sara, me and Glenn, in our idyll with the others, our family, coming in, going out.

I knew it was naive; I knew it was absurd. My bed would be in Sara's room, but when the dream deepened my bed would become Sara's bed, and because I didn't know where else to put him Glenn would be there too. And in my dream this was perfection. I had no other word for it. To be lying with Sara; perfection. To share her sleep, the warmth of her breath and the heat of her body, layer upon layer, the three of us, absorbed into one.

It eases my guilt, a little, if I tell myself that my dream, my desire, was *innocent*.

I just wanted to be with her always. I wanted to *know* her. I wanted to look at her, at all of her, at her body inside her clothes; the bits that didn't show: the bones of her shoulder blades, her hips, her elbows poking against the worn patches on her jumper; and at the bits that did show: the delicate blue underside of her wrists, the roughened skin of her knees and the soft, flat skin of her stomach, so carelessly revealed to me so often, every time she took off her jumper, got changed for PE or undressed in her room, throwing her clothes at the chair, dragging out others from underneath them. She took off her jumper like a boy, hands crossed, pulling it up from the hem, right up over her head, off both arms at once, so that her head popped out last, face pink and scuffed from the friction, hair crackling with static. And the skin around the small, finger-sized hole of her tummy button creased into little wrinkles as she bent forward, then tightened, taut as white muslin over her ribs as she stretched up her arms.

I wanted to look at her face all the time too, but I had to be careful here because I know I annoyed her. Two or three times she said to me, 'What are you staring at?' and I had to make some crack in reply, some quick comment to laugh it off and make *her* laugh. But still I had to look, at the way the tiny muscles under her skin moved as she talked, laughed, frowned. And at her eyes, her beautiful eyes; I could stare at her eyes forever and never see inside her soul.

13

I rapped on the back door with my fingers. No one answered, but I knew they were in there because the light was on and through the steamed-up glass of the door I could see shadows, big, distorted and grey. I rapped again; still no reply, so I turned the door handle with both hands – you had to really turn it pretty well all the way round because it was coming loose, so loose in fact that any day now it would turn right round and fall off altogether – and pushed the door open with my hip.

They were all in there, all except Rachel. *Sara and the boys*. It looked like a stage set, and they were all in their places, ready to go. That is how I saw it. I knew instantly that something had *happened*, something bad, yet it seemed like a show and they all had their parts; I crept in, looking for mine.

Mark was sprawled in a chair by the table, just inside the door. I almost tripped over his legs; he was stretched right out with his head tipped back. Glenn had pulled another chair right up beside Mark and was leaning over him, holding a wet cloth to his face. Next to him Sara was standing, tearing cotton wool from her make-up bag into small pieces, dropping them on to the table, busy, too busy even to look at me, to know that I was there. Andy was the only one who seemed to notice me come in. He was leaning with his back against the sink, arms folded, fingers of the left hand picking at the nails of the right. He nodded at me; I took this as my cue and sidled in and stood by him, in the small gap between him and Sara, as if there was a place there, for me.

It *was* like a stage set.

I took my place as if I was scripted in, and said, 'What's happened?' as if that was my line, but I must have timed it wrong or said it too quiet because no one answered, so I stepped forward, said it again.

Behind me Andy said, 'Rachel's step-dad caught them together.'

'Yes and nearly kicked the shit out of Mark.' Sara really *ripped* at the cotton wool as she spoke, throwing it on to the heap. 'Bastard,' she added and her breath fluttered the cotton wool about, blowing tufts of it off the pile.

'That's enough cotton wool, Sara,' Glenn said. 'Get some water. Get a bowl.'

Sara moved away from the table, started opening cupboards, found a Pyrex bowl and blew in it to clear the dust. She leant past Andy to fill it with water, pointedly shoving him out the way. Just as pointedly he ducked aside. Then he pulled his cigarettes out of his back pocket and held up the packet. 'Anyone want one?'

he asked, and I would have said yes but no one else did. Andy shrugged, lit one for himself anyway, squeezed round the others and opened the back door a bit, to let out the smoke.

Water sloshed out of the bowl when Sara banged it down on the table, soaking most of the cotton wool into a soggy mess. '*Fuck*,' she hissed. She seemed so *angry*. It seemed only Glenn's calm was holding her in.

'All right Sara,' he said, really quiet, and like a lamb she gathered up the wet lumps in her hand, squeezed the water back into the bowl and stood still, ready to help him.

The cloth under Glenn's hand had turned purple where it was pressed against Mark's eye. Water and watered-down pink rivulets of blood were running down Mark's cheeks. And tears too; suddenly I realized that hidden behind that rag Mark was *crying*, mouth open, breathing fast, almost shaking. The sight of him crying made me want to cry too, and my eyes prickled. I wanted to touch him, to hold his hand or something. Mark was just so sweet; he'd never hurt anyone. I couldn't bear to think of his lovely face all smashed up under that cloth. He was quite small, too, which made it worse; only a bully would hit someone small. Rachel's step-dad must be a total bastard.

In front of me, as if reading my mind, Sara said,

'Fucking bastard; I hate him. I fucking hate him and I wish he was fucking dead.'

With both hands, ever so carefully, and saying, 'All right, mate, it's all right,' Glenn eased the cloth away from Mark's face, just enough to get the cotton wool under. Mark started gasping with the pain, pressing the cloth back down with his own hands so that water from the cotton wool ran pink down his face. He pushed Glenn away, kicked with his legs and leant forward, sobbing, clutching his face. 'It's OK, mate,' Glenn said. 'It's OK.'

Sara sniffed loudly; Glenn dropped the cotton wool he was holding down on to the table; with that hand he held Mark's shoulder, rubbed at the leather of his jacket. With his other hand he reached out to Sara and stroked her back.

'He needs *stitches*,' Sara said and I could tell by her voice that she was crying too.

'I just want to go home,' Mark mumbled into his hands.

I couldn't stand it. 'Let me *do* something,' I said and stepped forward. Glenn's arm acted like a barrier, keeping me back.

'You can get some more water,' Sara said. 'We've got to clean his eye.' Glenn dropped his arm, barrier down, so I was standing between them. She shoved the bowl into my hands, shoved it so hard at me that it nearly spilt all over me. It looked like Ribena. I took the bowl to the sink, turned on the tap, rinsed it and rinsed it again till the last streaks of Mark's blood swirled away down the plughole.

With the bowl filled with clean water I turned around and I saw a look pass between Sara and Glenn that I would never be part of; I saw love and understanding of a kind that I would never know for myself. The bond between Sara and Glenn was far greater than anything that I could ever have with either of them, no matter how hard I tried. They were brother and sister, I was just the third one, the dispensable one. They didn't need me. They had each other.

'I'll take him home,' Glenn said and Sara just nodded her head. She didn't need to speak. Glenn understood anyway; I saw it on his face.

I stood behind them, redundant, with the bowl of water in my hand.

'Come on, mate.' Glenn patted Mark on the shoulder and started helping him to his feet. 'I'll take you home.'

Andy pushed the back door wide open and flicked his cigarette butt out into the night. 'I'll come with you, mate,' he said. He propped the door open with his foot and took Marks's other arm. Mark stood with his legs slightly bent; he leant heavily on Glenn, and shuffled to the door. It would take them forever to get him home.

'You girls be all right?' Glenn turned around and asked, just as they left. Sara nodded, and I nodded, making the tears that had been building up and balancing in my eyes drop out, and spill down my cheeks.

I wasn't jealous. It wasn't just that.

How could I be jealous when I needed them both? I couldn't have the one without the other. That was the thing. I needed them both and I needed them both to need me. I was in a triangle, all cornered up.

We stood in the kitchen, Sara and I, exactly as we were. I listened to the boys in the alley, up the side of the house, listened to them moving the bikes, working out who would take them and how. I heard their footprints on the pathway, fading, and then they were gone.

Then Sara turned to me and said, 'I don't know what you're crying for. Rachel's not your cousin.'

It was like a play, all of it. But they knew the script and I didn't. They all had their parts marked out and I had just muscled in, wanting to be in on it, wanting to belong. Now we were alone Sara turned on me, her first words an accusation, shutting me out, but I didn't care. I couldn't afford to care. We were alone. For the whole evening, I hoped, however sad I was for Mark.

'Let's go out,' I said, and she agreed. She relaxed once we were out, away from the house. All that hostility fell away and we linked arms as we walked, the way we used to, the way we hadn't done for ages. We walked through the rec to the High Street and down Station Road, to buy some fags at the off-licence. Then we came back the long way round, cutting across the allotments at the end of her road. It was a clear night, cold, with the faintest of mists clinging to the ground, making everything in the allotments seem spooky, the sticks stuck into the ground in rows, still mostly bare; the spikey clumps of plants tied back, and everywhere the smell of rotten cabbages. We huddled together, closer. Here and there were sheds; as we passed each one Sara tried the door to see if it would open. At last we found one that would and this seemed to cheer her up no end.

Inside it was pitch-dark of course, but she ran her hands along the shelf till she found a torch, an old tin one with a little stand to prop it up, the sort I imagine people used to take camping, years ago. It worked and she cast it about, into all the corners, over spades and and pots and bags of mud, and up over the shelf that ran all the way around the shed, stopping at the door. Looking closer among the clutter we found some matches that Sara took even though we didn't need them, a tin with packets of sugar lumps in, like you get in café's, which she stuffed in handfuls into her pockets, and another tin with an open packet of Rich Tea biscuits in. The biscuits were soft and not at all nice but we sat on upturned buckets and ate them anyway.

'We should have brought a drink with us,' I said. 'A nice little flask of cocoa.'

'You'd think there'd be a kettle or something, wouldn't you?' She sighed, a theatrical sigh. 'Some people have no consideration.'

Her face was a ghostly blue-white in the torchlight. We'd put the torch on the floor, balanced on its wonky stand, with the light pointed upwards. The batteries must have been old because the glare was fading already and every now and again it flickered. It was dead creepy, sitting there in the shadows. And cold, and very, very quiet, apart from us. 'Suppose someone comes?' I said, shivering from the cold, mostly.

'What, at this time of night?' Sara's voice was loud; anyone could have heard her, anyone lurking around outside. I shushed her as she spoke, gesturing with my hands but she didn't care. She carried on, even louder, 'They'll all be at home stuck in front of their tellies. Sat on their fat arses, snoring away.'

I couldn't help laughing, in spite of myself. 'They'll get a surprise tomorrow when they find their biscuits all gone.'

'Disgusting biscuits,' Sara said. 'Let's have a fag instead.'

The shed soon filled up with smoke, warming us, making us cosy. The torch kept flickering but my eyes were used to the dark now. We found ourselves quite at home.

'Are you all right now then?' I asked, eventually. I didn't want to get her upset again but I wanted her to know that I cared. I wanted us to share our problems; that's what friends are supposed to do, after all. And I hated it more than anything when she shut me out. 'Mark will be all right, won't he? And Rachel?'

'She better be. If Fat Ron so much as lays one little finger on her there'll be a queue of people lining up to get him, the bastard. I hate him.' She squashed her cigarette out as she said this, ramming it against the side of the bucket that she was sitting on. I couldn't see her face because she was leaning over, but in the dim light of the torch I could see her fingers bent hard and fierce, killing that butt. I watched as the remains of her cigarette split open against the metal and the insides fell out like soft hair. 'I'd like to get a carving knife and stick it in his big fat gut. But I can't,' she finished, letting go of the cigarette butt so that it fell down in the dark, lost somewhere on the dirt floor. 'We need his fucking money.'

There was so much anger in her voice. I used to believe that there was no such thing as hate, that it was just the other side of love, and trite things like that. I believed that you could dislike something very much, but not hate it. Hate is too full of feeling, and where there is feeling there is always something to be salvaged. Where there is feeling there has to be caring, and if you care, then so it follows that you can't hate. That was what I thought, before I met Sara. Now I know different. Now I know that hate is a very real thing, a very real and clean unbroken line, like mercury running through the core of all being. It ran through Sara; it *drove* her. Hate was a far greater force in Sara's life than love could ever be.

Sara *hated* Fat Ron, I know she did. It wasn't just about Rachel and Mark, it was about *Sara*, about the money and the unwilling neediness and the resentment and all the things that plaited her up inside.

I sat on my bucket, silent, wanting her to carry on, to tell me more. I wanted her to tell me everything, every little thing about her life and the thoughts inside her head but she didn't. Instead she said, 'I need a pee,' and stood up, and looked around the dark corners of the shed, and finally turned the bucket she'd been sitting on up the right way.

I clamped my hand over my mouth. 'Sara, you can't!'

'Yes I can. This will do nicely, thank you. All conveniences laid on.' She undid her jeans, pulled them down and squatted over the bucket, peeing noisily into the metal while I fell about laughing. 'Right,' she said when she'd finished. 'Now let's go home and have a nice cup of tea.'

* * *

The house was empty when we got back and I was glad; I could feel time slipping away, running away, and there I was with my arms outstretched, grasping, clinging on. We were cold from outside and the cold came in with us, making us sniff and breathe hard through our mouths. In the kitchen we made tea, both of us jiggling from one foot to the other while the kettle boiled, the steam hissing into the air, slowly warming us. Sara made the tea strong, poking at the teabags with a spoon, pressing them against the sides of the cups. Then she said, 'Hang on a minute,' and flicked the teabags out from the mugs and into the sink, and then picked up the cups and poured half of it all away. She dashed out the kitchen, into the dark hallway, flicking the lights on as she went, and was back in seconds with a bottle of Jack Daniels, which she tipped into the cups, filling them back up to the brim.

'Jesus, that's enough!' I giggled.

'Try it.' She picked up the mugs, handed me mine. 'Speciality of the house.'

Together we took a swig. It was horrible; cheap tea and milk on the turn and whiskey. I swallowed it down and thought for a moment it was going to come straight back up again.

Sara spat hers out, into the sink. 'Yuk! It's disgusting! How can you drink it? Must need more of this.' She slopped in some more whiskey.

I took another sip. This time the tea in it was less noticeable. 'It's still pretty awful,' I said, so she poured in some more.

My cheeks were beginning to feel numb and my mouth thick. 'D'you think they'll be coming back?' My voice came slow, sounding far off, even to myself. 'Glenn and Andy, I mean.'

'Don't know,' she said. 'Probably. Who cares? Still, we better take this upstairs.'

She took her cup and the bottle, and I followed her with my own cup and my bag with my overnight things, that I'd left down by the door.

Up in her room we chucked the remains of the tea out her window because it was so gross and decided we'd be better off just drinking the whiskey, neat. It was still early. We sat curled up on her bed, our faces hot from the drink. It was a while since I'd been in her bedroom. It smelt of socks and wool and damp heavy paper, slightly scented – the smell of the wallpaper I suppose, peeling away from the glue along the joins. At ten o'clock the phone rang and I dragged myself off the bed and back down the stairs.

'We're up in Sara's room,' I told my dad, trying to keep my voice from sounding thick. 'Having a cup of tea.'

She was lying down when I went back up, her face white and shadowed heavily around the eyes. She'd drunk too much whiskey. So had I, I suppose. Seeing her like that I let my own hold slip, and instantly I felt the room start to spin. I lay down beside her and stared with her at the ceiling. There was a big shadow on the ceiling, cast from the light bulb. As I stared it started to whirl round and round, faster and faster. I closed my eyes but then it seemed that *I* was moving, spinning around, so I opened them again and tried to focus.

Sara was quiet beside me but I felt the need to say something. It is a failing of mine; any great moment, any step on the ladder of time, and I have to mark it out with words.

'I wonder what we'll think,' I said, stupidly turfing out words, 'when we look back on this. I wonder if we'll remember this, in twenty years' time. I wonder where we'll be, then.'

Sara turned her head and looked at me as if I was an idiot. Her nose was almost touching mine. 'Fucking out of here,' she said. 'That's where I'll be.'

Soon after, Glenn came back, alone.

He called up the stairs. We lay where we were, heavy from drink, and didn't answer. He started coming up the stairs; hearing his footsteps I whispered, 'Sshh! Pretend we're asleep.' So we lay there silent until he went away, and we stayed like that till morning, fully clothed, stretched out on top of the covers, our heads swimming in the dark.

* * *

I wished her there forever. I wished her trapped, frozen in time and never changing. I wished her caught forever in that house, in the kitchen and the living room and in her bedroom and the small passageways in between, trapped forever, my prisoner, my Sara.

Like a butterfly on pins, I wanted her static. I wanted her mine.

14

You'd think someone had died, the way Sara moped about after the thing with Rachel and Mark happened. She could be moody at the best of times but that week she seemed sunk down in gloominess, swallowed up in it. Everything about her seemed dragged down. Oh I know what had happened was really terrible, but Sara couldn't seem to stop thinking about it for a minute. At least, I thought it was Mark and Rachel she was thinking about, though she never actually told me. She never actually said much at all. I did all the talking.

I talked about it on Monday on the way to school, going over what had happened, saying how awful it was.

'Has anything else happened?' I asked. 'Have you seen Rachel? How's Mark?'

But Sara just slumped along, head down, eyes staring at the pavement, mumbling yes and no and not much else. She only looked up when we walked past Rachel's house. Then she muttered, 'Bastard,' under her breath, and spat, just a little, on to the driveway, then hurried on again, head back down because Ron's car was still parked outside.

I talked about it at break too, up in the loos, and on

the way back to her house at lunchtime. I was trying to show that I cared. I *did* care, but with Sara you felt that you had to really prove it, all the time.

I thought the boys might come back to the house at lunchtime but they didn't. It was just us, just us all week. I should have been glad about that; I would have been glad about it but Sara was just so down. And so cold too. She didn't seem to care if I was there or not. She made tea, she made toast. We drank the tea, she ate the toast and we smoked our fags, and that was it. I had that feeling you get when you stand barefoot on a gravelly beach, right up by the water's edge, and the sea washes in and the sea washes out all around your feet and the sand beneath your toes moves too. You watch the sand moving, big bits of gravel among all the little bits, all moving at different speeds and although you don't move at all, although you stand perfectly still, you get that rushing feeling, as if the ground beneath you might all slide away. Like you are falling; that is how I felt.

I saw Mark, at school, in the playground. His eye was half-closed under the bruise and he'd got a big plaster stuck on the cut just above his cheek bone.

'Poor Mark,' I said to Sara. 'His poor eye.'

And I kept asking after Rachel. 'How's Rachel?' I'd ask, again and again, in the most caring, concerned voice that I could manage.

And again and again in reply I just got the coldest, briefest, 'Fine.'

Sara needed me to prove that I cared; that's how it was. That's what I thought. So I tried very, very hard and I thought I was doing a pretty good job of it, after all it is not easy being endlessly nice and kind and not biting back when all you get in return for your efforts is a cold, cold shoulder. I trotted along beside her, feeling like a dog being kicked, kicked, kicked, saying things like, 'Maybe Ron'll let Rachel out if it's just to see us,' and, 'What about at lunchtime – maybe Mark could cycle over to her school at lunchtime, see her then . . .'

But obviously I got it all completely wrong because on the Friday of that week she turned round to me and snapped, 'For God's sake can't you just shut up about Rachel. *Rachel, Rachel, Rachel*, like she's all you care about and she's not even your fucking cousin.'

I stared at her, stunned by the injustice. *Sara, Sara, I care about you.*

The rain was plastering her fringe into flat clumps on her forehead; droplets of rain hovered down the strands, quivering on the ends where they met with her eyelashes. It was a miserable, miserable day. So grey and so wet with the clouds so low you couldn't raise your head. The only colour in such bleakness was the glare of Sara's eyes, bright with anger, and with something else that hurt me right in my chest.

She looked as if she hated me. How could she? I was her *friend*.

This was lunchtime. We stood in an alleyway up the side of the houses opposite the school, hoping I suppose that standing between the two walls would somehow shelter us from the rain. It didn't of course. It took ages to light our fags, taking it in turns to arch our hands over the match while the other one puffed and puffed, trying to get a light. I relished this; it seemed like tenderness. It seemed like she cared while she took so much trouble to get my cigarette going, and I treasured this, this little act that so belied the look in her eyes.

'I'm *sorry*,' I said. 'I was only asking. Only trying to show I care.'

'God, you always come it so hurt, don't you?' she snapped. 'Always the poor little me.' She bumped her shoulder against the wall and took several hard drags on her cigarette, as if she really needed it. In between drags she chewed on lips as thin and pale as an old woman's. 'Can't say anything without you getting the hump—'

'Oh Sara, come on, that is so unfair!' Outrage made my voice rise high and squeaky.

'Or without getting a fucking *lecture*.' She bit the words out, so angry and so tense that the muscles in her neck had hollowed just below her jaw. 'Why don't you just get off my fucking back for five minutes? Rachel is fine. Mark is fine. Everyone is fine. Just don't put yourself out worrying about me.'

She flicked her fag butt so it landed in the puddles by my feet, and turned away from me and stomped off on her own back to school.

I stayed there on my own for a while, in that alleyway in the rain, getting wet. I smoked my cigarette till it had burnt right down to my fingertips then I let the soggy butt fall, *plop*, on to the wet pavement, where it landed by Sara's. Two old cigarette butts, rocking slightly, getting hammered by the rain.

I leant back against the wall and let the rain hit my face and run down in random pathways, into my mouth and out again. It stung my eyes; I closed them tight and then opened them again, letting it sting them some more.

When you hurt, really hurt, you feel it throughout your body. It starts in your middle and spreads out, down your thighs and into your arms. Oh it is so easy to say this now but that was the start of the end, when she turned away from me. That was when I started losing Sara.

When school finished that day she was already in the playground when I came out, arguing with Andy. Having a go at *him* now. She spat like a cat in a fight, arms and legs rigid, head angled forwards, hissing out her anger. I stood by the entrance, not sure if I was waiting for her or if I was afraid to walk past. I could hear what they were saying. Everyone could.

'Well do you want me to come round or not?' Andy said. He kind of laughed as he spoke, though clearly he was annoyed; the smile on his face was fixed, lop-sided, caught stiff in anger.

'I don't fucking care do what you like,' Sara snapped, all in one sentence, and Andy stepped back and ducked slightly as if dodging a blow.

'Fine,' he said. 'I'll take that as a no, shall I?'

Sara shrugged, said, 'Please yourself.'

Andy threw his arms wide in frustration, in disbelief, and half-shouted, 'God, Sara, what is your problem?'

'You are!' Sara shouted back. She slung her bag down on the ground near his. It had stopped raining but the ground was wet and it landed smack in a puddle and skidded across the gravel. 'You are my problem!' she spat at him, kicking at the air in front of him with her foot. 'You're such a fucking loser!'

'No –' Andy stepped towards her now, pointing his finger at her, anger flushing dark across his face '– you're the loser, Sara. Nothing's good enough for you, is it? Nothing.' He jabbed that finger at the air in front of her, hard, ramming home the words. 'And let me tell you something, Sara. You carry on like this and you'll end up all on your own. You know that? All on your fucking own.'

Still she had to have the last word. 'Fuck off,' she shouted so the whole world could hear. Then she grabbed her bag up from the wet ground, slung it back over her shoulder and stormed off, out the gates, and Andy kicked his bag, picked it up and walked off the other way, towards the bike sheds.

I was *glad*.

I was glad that Andy had said those things. After all it was true, every word of it. She had it coming. It was what I wanted to say to her sometimes but *I* never had the guts.

I just hoped she'd listened. I hoped his words had gone right in and hit that thing inside her head that made her push us all away.

Even so, I saw my chance then, and I took it. I ran after her, calling, 'Sara, wait, Sara are you OK?' like the hypocrite that I am. She didn't stop so I kept on running, until I caught up with her going down the road opposite the gates.

'Are you OK?' I said again, puffed now from running. 'I heard what Andy said . . .'

But Sara wasn't angry any more, Sara was crying, staring straight ahead as she walked, tears dripping off her eyelashes like the rain had at lunchtime, mouth crooked with sorrow. And all those little worms of disloyalty inside me withered. I *was* Sara's friend. Her true, true friend. Me, only me, always, I'd be there, no matter what. Nothing would change that, ever. I so wanted to believe that. I put my arm around her shoulders and she let me, she didn't shrug me away, so I walked with her like that, with my arm around her, and I said all these things, all these soothing things that I so, so wanted to be true. I said, 'Take no notice, Sara, he's just a bloke; he's not worth it. When it comes down to it it's your friends that count. I'm your friend, Sara; I'm your friend, I'll never treat you like that, Sara, never . . .'

But I don't know if it made any difference.

She let me keep my arm around her and she let me keep on talking. But she didn't say anything back. She cried in a steady stream, unbroken, with her mouth slightly open and the sobs coming out in a faint continuous moan. I have never seen anyone else cry the way Sara did. She cried like death, like that groaning at the end; she gave herself up entirely.

When we got to her house she stood still, with her hands hanging down by her sides and her head bent over, still sobbing. And I stood there too, with my arm around her; I turned so that I could put my other arm around her and I held her. She bent her head against my shoulder and I held my arms around her back. She seemed so pliant, so soft now. I let my hands stroke the back of her denim jacket, up and down; lightly, so lightly. I couldn't have held her tight; she felt so fragile, so tragic in my arms.

She let me hold her; that is the thing. That is what I didn't want to end. I didn't want to go into her house with her because Glenn was in there and I didn't want to see him. Not now. But I didn't want to go on home yet either. I didn't want to break away; I wanted to stay right there, holding her, forever. To me this seemed like some great important moment; I couldn't let it end. I felt that something else should happen, that something should be said. I felt as if I'd taken a step backwards on the inevitable path towards losing Sara and I wanted to take a second, and a third. I couldn't let her go.

So we stood like that on the path outside her house for a long time. Sara stopped crying. The groaning wound down, like she'd run out of energy. She stood with her face still buried in my shoulder and then she spoke, at last. 'I just wish everyone would get off my fucking back,' she said.

I guess she was so fed up that she just didn't care if she went indoors or if she stayed out there in the cold, listening to me banging on.

Later I realized I'd probably been doing what she'd accused me of at lunchtime: lecturing her.

* * *

She still expected Andy to turn up, on Saturday night.

When I got to their house she was in the kitchen. She'd forced open the window and she was leaning against the sink, smoking a fag. In her hand she held a small plate with two dead butts on it and a load of ash. She was wearing that top, the one we'd nicked. The one *I'd* nicked. There was no way in a million years I could ever have taken it home with me, so on the bus back home that day I'd pulled it out from under my jacket, and said, 'You have it.'

'No, you wanted it,' she'd said back.

But I'd insisted, I'd pushed it at her, made her take it. 'Go on, you have it. Then we both have something, one each.'

She'd shrugged, and taken it.

It was too tight across the chest. As she moved the buttons gaped, showing the grey of her bra through the gaps. She'd got a lot of make-up on too and she was wound up, waiting, waiting, though of course she said she wasn't. She stubbed out her cigarette, bashing it into the plate.

'Glenn's in the front room,' she said and I followed her through. Then we sat there in the living room, the three of us, uncomfortable under the weight of her tension.

Eventually Glenn said, 'Well, what did you expect?'

And Sara jumped up and said, 'Sod this. I'm going round Rachel's.'

Glenn put his arm around me when she'd gone, and I slipped down a bit so I fitted under his armpit and I crossed my legs, woman-like. He stank of aftershave and he was wearing his black shirt, the one he usually wore on Saturday nights.

Something I noticed in that short time is that at first he was like an animal, intent, so driven by his own lust that his eyes clouded blind; he worked on me like an animal at its prey. But after a little while, after a few weeks or so, when he'd had me a few times, some other effect came into play ... *romance* I suppose. He'd start on me but then he'd stop and lie still for whole minutes, just stroking my hair. Or he'd stare into my eyes, his own eyes murky with emotion. He'd dabble his hands across my cheeks and he'd kiss me, then he'd stop suddenly and just hold me, as if that was enough.

I hated it when he did that. I hated it when he looked deep into my eyes. I didn't want him to see what was in there. And I didn't want to know what was inside him.

I preferred it when he just grabbed at my clothes and I didn't have to think. It was OK if I didn't have to think. I could cope then. But this *love* bit was all too heavy; it felt too much like guilt to me.

I said I loved him because he said it to me. He stared at me, he said it, and I forced myself to say it back. I had to; he was Sara's brother. And when I said it he lay still for a while with me pulled down against him and he stared at the ceiling. Like it took a while for it to sink in.

We sat on the sofa, Glenn and me, like couples do, and he kissed me once or twice, the soppy kisses of coupledom and I did my best to like it. But the minute I heard Sara come in the back door and run upstairs to her room I saw it as my chance to bolt.

'I'll go,' I said. 'See she's OK.'

I tapped on her door and walked straight in.

Glenn's aftershave was strong up my nose still; I rubbed at it with my hand till through the heavy scent I could smell Sara, her room, the space that surrounds her. It was a smell that made me want to sleep, like heaven.

I nearly asked her how Rachel was, but stopped myself just in time. Instead I stood just inside the doorway and blurted out, 'I'm going soon. My dad'll be here at half past ten,' and that put the boundaries up for anything we might say; it put a time limit on our pain, for tonight.

She was standing by the chest of drawers, fiddling with the bottles and things on the top there; she squeezed pink gunk out of a tube and on to a cotton wool pad, and started to wipe it over her eyes. She looked so pissed off; the corners of her mouth turned right down as she scrubbed at her skin with that cotton wool. In the dim, orange-brown light of her room she looked more like fifty than fifteen.

'If you're upset about Andy,' I said, 'why don't you just phone him? Just say you're sorry.'

'Because I'm not sorry.' She turned her head a little and dragged the cotton wool ball slowly down her cheek; even in that light I could see the contrast, see the clean child-white skin, wiped bare. 'Why should I be sorry? He's been getting on my nerves for ages.'

I moved towards her a little and stood so that I could see her face in the mirror. I could see her, and I could see myself behind her, back a little, like a shadow, like the background to the light that is Sara. 'Don't you want to make it up with him?'

'No.' The cotton wool ball was dirty now, all smeary pink and orange and black. She tore it open with both hands, gluing the sticky bits together in her fingers so that the inside fluffed out, proud and unused. Then she picked up that tube again and squeezed, piling it on, round and round in a little peak, like strawberry sauce on ice cream.

I didn't believe her so I said, 'But you can't just leave it like that. I mean, *you* told *him* to fuck off, remember.'

'So?' Our eyes met in the reflection. You could never tell anything from Sara's eyes. She kept them blank, cold; she gave nothing away. The eyes are not the window to the soul, not with Sara, oh no. Holding my stare she raised the cotton wool to her face again, and wiped it back across her skin. 'I was going to ditch him anyway.'

'Don't you care about anyone?' The words were out before I could stop them. Instantly I felt the heat buzzing in my cheeks and my ears. 'Don't you *care?*'

Sara stopped what she was doing. She held my gaze in the reflection and then, still staring, she threw the dirty cotton wool down on to the top of the drawers among all the bottles and tubes and junk. 'What the fuck has it got to do with you?'

She was just so cold. 'You just don't seem to care . . .' I could feel my voice wobbling, bubbling up. I swallowed hard, trying to keep it steady. 'Sara, I don't understand you. Why are you being like this? I can't *talk* to you anymore. You've changed . . .'

She turned around now, and faced me for real. 'It's not me that's changed,' she spat. 'It's you. You think you're so fucking important just because you're screwing my brother.'

'What's wrong?' Glenn kept saying but I couldn't stop crying. I expect he was hoping to fuck me in the ten minutes or so before my dad came for me, or feel me up at least, and normally I would have let him. But I couldn't stop crying and I couldn't begin to say why, so

I just sat next to him on the sofa and cried till half past ten. Then I swallowed up my tears and forced my face back in check, went outside to my dad's car, and went home.

Sara didn't wait for me on Monday morning. I didn't even bother to call for her because I knew she'd have already gone on, and I was right. The bell rang just as I got to school, and when I walked into tutorial she was already there, sitting slouched over her bag, back turned half-away from me, hair falling over her face like a shield between us.

I sat down in my place and I could smell her. I could smell every room of her house on her skin and her clothes, I could smell the toast she'd cooked that morning and the cigarette she'd smoked on the way to school. I could even smell the chips and the bacon she'd fried last night, the memory of hot fat still clinging to her hair.

There are two ways of crying, I think. There is the usual sort with the red eyes and the sobbing and all that, and then there's the other sort, the rarer sort that swells like a massive lump in the chest and throat, so hot that you can't swallow and so filled with tears that no sobbing is needed at all. The tears come fast, one on top of the other. No effort is required, no audience. I cried like that once before when I was just seven, the Monday morning after my rabbit died and my dad had told me to ask my teacher if she wanted Butch's straw and food for the class hamster. I couldn't tell my teacher; instead I sat at my desk in silence with the tears running in streams down my face.

I cried like that now. The lump in my throat was so hot I knew what was going to happen and dipped my head. Tears splashed on to the desk. So many it grew wet and I wiped at them with my sleeve and sat back slightly, head as bent as possible. Tears ran down my face, my neck, into the collar of my top. I picked at a thread on the cuff of my cardigan and tried to wipe my face on my shoulder.

No one sees, when you cry like that. Even the person you love, sitting right beside you doesn't see when you cry like that.

The sleeve of my jumper was wet where I'd wiped my face on it, and the ink smudged under my hand as I wrote. It didn't matter. It was a stupid letter anyway. Apologies again, and what was I apologizing for? Why me always? Sara, I'm sorry, sorry, sorry. Sorry for everything I've ever done. Sorry for everything I haven't done. Sorry that I'm always *sorry*.

I had a deep hollow feeling inside, a sense of giving something up. *Sorry, sorry, sorry*, I scribbled. It means everything and it means nothing. I pulled the cuff of my jumper down over my hand and rubbed at the words, smearing them into blue nothingness. I screwed up the piece of paper and started again.

Are you talking to me? I wrote this time, and pushed the paper across the desk, under her nose.

She looked at it. I thought she would just shove it back at me or ignore it. But she took a biro out of her pencil case. *Don't know*, she scribbled back.

I tore another piece of paper from the back of my exercise book, bigger this time. *Well write to me instead while you make your mind up*, I wrote and slid it across the desk.

She didn't look at me but under her hair, I saw her lips flicker into the tiniest of smiles. She didn't write anything, though, so I pulled the note straight back. I wasn't giving up now. *What about you and Andy?* I wrote, and passed it back again.

He's a bastard, she wrote now, underlining the word 'bastard' three times with her pen.

Well he can't help that, I replied. *He's a bloke.*

And that was the right thing, for Sara. We were OKish, again, for now.

It was challenge, challenge, challenge. Each of us, holding on to different sticks, not letting go. On the end of Sara's stick were the strings that worked me like a puppet, dancing to her lead. The stick I held was the stick a dog holds, between its teeth, gripping on out of loyalty, out of love.

15

There was a party that Saturday, at some Year Eleven bloke's house, in the road that leads down past the railway line. The boy was in Glenn's class. He was one of the grungers; there was a whole gang of them in Year Eleven. Glenn said they had brilliant parties, these blokes, really wild.

My mum and dad would never have let me go, so there was no point in even asking. The only way I could go was if I stayed the night at Sara's, and it was hard enough just getting them to let me do that these days. So I laid it on dead thick. I said, 'Sara's mum's going to be out till late and her brother too, and Rachel's going to come round, and Sara's mum said wouldn't it be nice if I could come too and stay over and we could watch films and make popcorn,' and so on and so on. I conjured up quite a picture. They couldn't be so mean as to say no.

And when my dad dropped me off at Sara's house I said in my sweetest voice, 'Don't phone at ten o'clock, Dad. There's a film on TV and you'll ruin it if you phone right in the middle of it.'

My dad flicked the interior light in the car on and

looked at me. I looked back, all innocence. 'Well what time does the film finish?' he asked.

'Ten-thirtyish, I think,' I said, reluctantly, wishing he'd say *OK, I won't phone you at all.*

'Then I'll phone you at ten-thirty,' he said. 'On Sara's phone.' Meaning on the house phone, of course. Just in case I dared to go out.

No one answered when I banged on the back door, but they were expecting me so I pushed it open and went on in. I called out *Hi* and I could hear them upstairs, in their separate rooms, both getting ready to go out.

I ran on up and I went into Sara's room.

She'd got a tub of red gel that you could put in your hair to give yourself streaks.

'You just slap it on with your fingers,' she said. 'Dead easy.'

I watched as she rubbed cochineal red into her beautiful amber hair. She peered at herself in the mirror, frowning in concentration. Very carefully she worked through the front sections of her hair, holding each section up in turn with one hand and sticking the other hand into the tub, scooping out blood-red gloop, transferring it to her head and smearing it down the strands. It oozed through her fingers and ran down the back of her hands as she squeezed it into her hair, making sure she'd got the whole length covered, rubbing it into her scalp at the roots and spreading it all the way down to the ends.

It was a bit more hit-and-miss at the back where she couldn't see. She missed all the roots at the back and all the ends. It looked awful.

'There,' she said, staring at her reflection. 'What do you think?'

'It's good,' I lied.

'Not too much?' She tipped her head sideways, forward, sideways again, surveying her work in the mirror.

'No,' I lied again, though I couldn't help adding, 'but I think you've got lovely hair anyway.'

'Bit boring though. Looks better now.' Her hands were stained with red juice, like she'd been picking strawberries and crushing them with her fingers. 'Let's put some on you.'

'Oh no, I don't know. My dad'd go nuts.'

'We'll just do a little bit,' she insisted. 'It washes straight out.'

So I stood by the mirror while she pulled her sticky fingers through my hair. Luckily, I'm so dark you could hardly notice it.

'It's probably meant for blondes,' I said.

'Mmm.' She was disappointed. She tilted her head, considering me. 'You could wear more make-up though.'

'I've got eyeliner on.'

'Yes but not much.' She wiped her fingers on

some cotton wool, pulling the threads off as they stuck to her skin. 'Go on, let me put some of mine on you. It *is* a party.' She tipped blue liquid from one of her bottles on to a piece of cotton wool and handed it to me. 'Take your eyeliner off,' she said, 'and I'll do you up properly.'

I sat on the bed and she tipped out her make-up bag beside me, spreading out the bottles, tubes, pencils and broken compacts so she could see what she'd got. There was enough stuff to paint up a whole brothel of whores.

'Trust me,' she said, but I couldn't trust her entirely so I held on to a little hand mirror, so that I could see what she was doing.

First she squeezed pink foundation on to the back of her hand, then she daubed it on to my olive skin where it stood out in streaks. 'It's not *quite* the right colour for you,' she said as she smeared it with her red fingers, rubbing and rubbing to try and blend it together. 'But it'll look all right in the dark. You've got to set it with powder.' She opened a compact, carefully, so the contents didn't go everywhere. There wasn't much of the powder left and what there was had broken up a bit in the tray. She ground the dirty-looking sponge into the loose bits then pressed it on to my face, all over. I could feel my skin tightening up.

'Now a little blusher,' she said and creamed it on with her fingertips, making my now pink cheeks even pinker. 'D'you want eye shadow?' She flicked through all the little pots and compacts, opening them, checking their colours. 'What d'you reckon? Dark grey? Gold?' She stared at my eyes, sizing up their colour, their prospects, and I stared back at hers, doing the same. 'This one,' she decided, picking up a little pot of dark, sooty-grey. 'Same as me.' Then came the eyeliner again, only she said you get a much darker line with liquid. 'Except it's much harder doing it on someone else,' she muttered, biting into her lip as she concentrated. With the mascara she gave me the stick and said, 'Do it yourself. I'm not even going to try.'

I took the wand from her hand, globbed it on to my lashes and just stared into the mirror. Flushed and black-eyed my reflection stared back, amazed. I looked . . . *bold.*

In an odd way I liked it.

Suddenly I burst out laughing and flopped down on to my back, straight on top of all that make-up, but I didn't care.

'What d'you reckon then?' Sara asked, grinning at me. 'But don't forget your lipstick.' She twisted hers up, coloured her own mouth till it was shiny and red as a new fire engine, then plopped down the tube so it landed square on my chest. It was warm from her hand when I picked it up. Still lying down I held up the mirror and drew a tart's smile on to my face to match her own.

'Right then,' Sara said. 'I'll call Glenn and we'll go.'

I didn't want to get up. I wanted to stay there longer, like that. Suddenly it seemed a shame that we were going to a party at all and couldn't just stay messing around in her room all evening.

'I've got to be back by ten-thirty,' I said, suddenly remembering. 'My dad's phoning, to check I'm here. Still, I suppose you don't have to come back then.' I wanted her to say *Of course I'll come back with you,* or better still, *Let's not bother going to the party, let's just stay and have a laugh here.* But she didn't. She picked up her fags from the dressing table, opened the door and yelled for Glenn.

'Can I stay in here with you tonight?'

It was out before I could think.

I didn't mean anything by it, only that it was so cosy, just the two of us alone like that but Sara turned in the doorway and gave me the weirdest look.

'I don't think my brother will like that much, do you?' she said.

Sara went on down the stairs and I followed her; Glenn's door opened and he clattered down behind us and *wham*, the whole mood had changed.

Sara's mood had changed.

'Ah, isn't that sweet?' she sneered as Glenn kissed me on the mouth.

'Leave it out, Sara,' Glenn said, irritated. I started to pull away from him but he held me back beside him, keeping his arm around my waist. We were in the hall; in that small, dim space I was stuck, squashed up against Glenn while Sara stood facing us with her arms folded across her chest. Everything about her was hostile now. I didn't know if I should stay where I was or break free of Glenn and attach myself to her instead. I hesitated and stayed where I was.

Sara tutted in exasperation '*Excuse* me,' she said, and pushed past us.

She picked up a pair of shoes from down by the front door; they were her mother's shoes, black pointed stilettos with lots of straps. They were a little too small for Sara's feet but she squeezed them on anyway. As she stooped over to do up the straps her top rode right up her back, baring her marble-white skin and the nobbles of her spine.

Glenn and I stood there, waiting, watching.

'You know Andy'll be there tonight, Sara,' Glenn said.

'So?' she mumbled, still struggling with those straps.

'I'm just saying.'

'Well you don't need to.' She stood up now, flicking her hair back out of her eyes and pulling her top back down into place.

Glenn took his arm away from me then. He moved towards her a little, but only a little; she had *keep back* written all over her. 'All right, Sara,' he said. 'I just wanted to make sure you know.'

'Why?' she demanded. 'Do you think I should stay at home, then? Weeping into my pillow?' She squared up to him like she was expecting a fight. 'Do you think the very sight of him will be too much for me?'

Annoyance flushed red across Glenn's cheekbones. 'Just cool it, Sara. I don't want any trouble.'

She snorted. 'What do you think I'm going to do? Beat him up?'

'Don't be stupid.'

'You're being stupid,' Sara shouted, and she was staring at me now. 'You just don't want me around, crowding you out. Well you needn't worry. I don't intend playing gooseberry to you two all night.'

She didn't even put a jacket on and it was freezing out. She just slammed out the back door leaving us to follow and stomped ahead with her arms folded tight across her middle to keep out the cold, fingers biting into her upper arms. She walked in big strides; too big for her short, tight skirt and the split up the back strained with every step. The split went right up to the top of her thighs, but it hadn't always been like that. You could see where it had grown over time, the seam gradually unravelling, fraying along the edges.

I wanted to talk to her and sort things out but Glenn had me by the hand, tight, keeping me back with him. 'Leave her,' he said. 'Let her calm down.'

So we walked the ten minutes or so to Jake Mann's house in silence, Sara staying ahead, heels *clack, clack, clacking* on the pavement. The sound reverberated through the still, cold air, like hammers on metal. She must have been half-frozen. Her shoulders and back were rigid inside the thin material of her top, taut against her anger and the cold. Every now and again the wind blew at her hair enough for me to see that the label inside the back of her collar was sticking up. I stared at this, totally miserable.

Garfield Lane was a long road with little terraced houses all down one side. On the other side of the road was a high fence and the railway line. Jake Mann's house was right down the end, next to a disused storage yard. You could hear the music from way up the street, and when we got to the house there were people out in the front garden and on the pavement, blokes mostly, already off their heads. One guy was lying out on the pavement outside the house, unconscious apparently, and someone had been sick on the pathway. We stepped over this and went into the house.

It was crowded already and the music was thumping out, really loud once you were inside. Sara disappeared straight away and Glenn ran upstairs to dump our jackets. I waited for him at the bottom of the stairs. The house had those stairs that go straight up from the front door, boxed in with a wall on both sides so they seem really narrow. Someone had scraped most of the paper off those walls like they were going to decorate, someday, when they got round to it. Here and there the little bits that were left curled away from the walls in strips, like bunting at a fair.

The living room was packed out and Glenn pulled me through to the kitchen, to get a beer. He'd brought some cans and he broke one off for both of us then dumped the rest on the side, with all the other drink. The beer had got shaken about, walking there, and it frothed out of my can when I opened it; quickly I stepped back to stop it going all over me and it spilled on to the floor instead. I put my hand over the opening, then I put the can to my mouth and drank the froth down.

Andy was there before us and when he saw us he worked his way over to us, pushing through the crowd.

'Sara with you, mate?' he asked Glenn.

'She was.' Glenn swigged from his can. 'But I warn you, mate, she's in a fucking awful mood.'

We followed Andy into the living room. It was dark and crammed with people, Year Eleven mostly, some older by the look of them, drinking, smoking, shouting over the music. We heard Sara before we saw her; heard her laugh cutting high over all the other noise. She was on the other side of the room flirting with one of the grungers, a bloke called Simon Leevy. We watched as she took the can from his hand and drank from it, tossing back her hair as she handed it back. He had a spliff in his other hand and he held it for her to take a puff, getting right up close and putting his fingers to her lips. She took a long, slow drag then blew the smoke out into his face, slowly. There were other boys hanging around her too but it was Simon's arm that her hand was on, Simon's face that her own face was thrust into, laughing. It was Simon that she was draped all over like a whore.

'Fuck this, mate, I'm out of it,' Andy said and pushed his way outside. Glenn followed him so I had to as well; back out the front door into the cold foggy air, careful not to tread on that pile of sick.

'Fuck her! Fuck her!' Andy screwed up his can and flung it back at the house. Glenn put his arm out to him, to calm him, but Andy pushed him off, right away from him. 'She may be your sister, mate,' he said and he kicked at the ground, 'but I am fucking out of this.'

He stormed off. Glenn said, 'Wait here,' to me and ran after him. Andy was way down the street already, walking in the middle of the road. Glenn caught him up and stopped him; again Andy pushed him away. I could hear them shouting from there but not what they were saying.

It was freezing cold out there and I shivered without my jacket. I didn't know what to do. I felt like a total prat, just standing there. They were gone for ages so eventually I went back inside the house to find Sara. I thought I'd talk to her, to try and sort things out. We couldn't leave things like that. I couldn't leave *her* like that, taking everything out on everyone, and acting so wild, like she was teetering on a cliff, about to fall.

I pushed my way into the living room but Sara wasn't there any more; I squeezed through to the kitchen but she wasn't there either. Some people had gone out the back, into the garden, but not Sara. I couldn't find her anywhere.

I got myself a beer and stood by the back door and drank it; then another. Glenn would be back in a minute; he wouldn't just leave me there.

There was no one else at the party that I knew. They were all Year Eleven or older, apart from Sara and me. I wished Glenn would hurry up and come back. I stood on my own in my spot talking to no one, sipping from my can till the smell of it made me feel sick and the misery started turning to anger, and I couldn't stand it any longer. I just wanted to go, though

I didn't know where I could go. I couldn't exactly turn up at home and explain it to Mum and Dad, but I couldn't go back to their house either without Sara or Glenn.

I shoved my way back down the hall, past shoulders and backs, but still no sign of Glenn, still no sign of Sara, so I went upstairs to hunt through the piles of coats and jackets for my own. My head was pounding – I didn't know what to do, I couldn't just *leave* but I didn't want to go back downstairs on my own again either. I opened one of the other doors, flicked on the light–

I saw the sole of her foot first. I saw the sole of Sara's foot as she lay half-naked on the bed in front of me underneath Simon Leevy. I saw the sole of her foot and her leg, bare, raised and wrapped around his. He was leaning right over her, one hand pushing down his trousers and the other grabbing at her knickers, jamming his filthy groping fingers into her, poking at her flesh. He had his hand where I wanted to touch her, on that sweet, sweet place at the very top of her leg where her bottom began. That place where the skin was so soft and so white and ever so slightly pimply, just like it was on the backs of her arms, just above the elbow. He had his hand right there where I wanted to touch her – but *I* would never *dig* at her like that, *I* would never snatch and claw. Oh no, *I* would trail my fingers over her skin like it was silk. Gently I would touch her, so very, very gently. I would stroke her, *stroke* that sweet pink skin inside, I would—

'*What the fuck are you staring at?*' she screeched at me, sitting up, hair messed, eyes burning.

Sick scalded my throat, filled my mouth and my chest heaved – I clamped my hand over my mouth but it spilt through my fingers, down my sleeve, and I ran out the room, got to the bathroom and let it all come – not real sick, just liquid, loads of it, splashing into the sink and running sticky down my chin. It bubbled out of my nose too and from my eyes, tears mixing with it all, and I sobbed and choked and spat it all out, turning on the taps full blast to drown out the sound, till there was nothing left, nothing at all, and I hung there and watched it all run away down the drain.

They were probably still in the bedroom. Probably doing it by now.

Someone was banging on the door, hard. Glenn's voice called, 'Kate? You in there, Kate? Anyone seen Kate?'

I turned the taps off. In the mirror my face was red, streaky. Black had smeared down my cheeks and out from the sides of my eyes and into my wet, matted hair I cleaned all that make-up off with loo roll, all of it, so then I just looked blotched and puffy but at least I didn't look like a whore.

* * *

Glenn was in the hall.

'There you are,' he said, when I came back down the stairs. 'What the fuck is going on?' He looked at my face, looked at my eyes and my cheeks, red, scrubbed bare. 'Andy's pissed off somewhere. Can't find you. Can't find Sara—'

'Sara's upstairs having it off with Simon Leevy.' Oh they sounded so cold, those words, so empty, even to my own ears. I knew I was being dramatic again but I just felt so *felled*, and as I said those cheap, sordid words I could imagine them up there, still in that room, imagine what they were doing now, how far they'd gone on. I could see it in my head, the progress; I could see that boy's back and his arse, humping away on top of her, smothering her, dirtying up her skin with his stinking male sweat.

Glenn stared at me, then he stared up the stairs, and anger swept dark red all over his face.

'I'll kill her,' he said. 'I'll fucking kill her . . .'

I started crying then, really crying, though I was surprised there were any tears left to come out. He put his hands on my arms. He wanted to go and find Sara but my tears stopped him. I couldn't let him go up there, I couldn't let him barge in on them, saying *Kate told me you were up here, Kate told me what you were doing.* I knew I'd never forget what I'd seen, but I wanted her to forget that I'd seen it. Or at least to forget the way I'd just stood there and stared.

'I want to go,' I said to him. 'Please, I just want to go.'

He hesitated, looked up the stairs, looked at me . . .

'I'm going,' I said and I pushed past him, out the front door and on to the street so that he had to follow, and I just let myself carry on crying because that was easier than talking. He walked beside me with his arm round my shoulders muttering *Shit* and *I don't fucking believe this* and *I'll fucking kill her* till his anger abated and then he was silent.

Back at their house I stood in the kitchen, still sniffing, while he fiddled about with the gas and stuck the kettle on for tea. Then he pulled me over to him and held me in his arms.

'Sara can be one fucking bitch,' he said. 'She can't fuck around with my mates like that.' He lifted my chin with his hand, traced a finger under my eye where tears were still trickling out. 'But why are you so upset?'

His eyes were exactly like hers, light turquoise-green, yet they weren't cold like hers, they weren't hard; and his skin was like hers too, so very white, only on him it didn't stay that way, on him it flushed pink across his neck and his cheekbones with anger and with passion, flushed across his chest too; and I wanted to see it, see him warm for me where she was so cold, so I kissed him, and I put my hands up inside his shirt so I could feel his skin, feel his warmth. And then he was kissing me back, hard into my mouth, pulling me tight up against him, and his hands were inside my jacket, working their way round to my chest – but what I wanted was for him to touch me the way Simon Leevy had touched Sara so I pressed myself against him, put my hands on his backside, pressed harder and then he groaned and instantly his hands were there, up my skirt, feeling me through my tights, and I could hardly breathe.

The kettle started to hiss and he moved to pull away, but I didn't want him to so I carried on kissing him, and he reached behind him to take the kettle off the gas, then his hands were back and it was like instant fire and I wanted more, I wanted everything *she* had, *now*, I wanted to know what *she* felt like.

Still holding me, still with his fingers grabbing at me, he started pulling me towards the door, then we were upstairs on the bed, and I wanted to lie just like she was, and then he was on top of me and I let my eyes half-close so that my vision blurred, and it was Sara I was seeing. Sara in my arms, in my body, Sara hot within me, holding me . . .

And when the phone rang at ten-thirty I got out of Glenn's bed and pulled on Glenn's shirt and went down to answer it.

'Hello, Dad,' I said into the dark. 'We were just in the kitchen making toast.' The carpet was gritty under my naked feet and I shivered, damp from Glenn's sweat, his dirty sweat, all over my skin. 'I'll be back about ten in the morning,' I said, little Katie that I should be, good little Katie, eating popcorn, watching films. 'I'll walk unless it's raining, OK?'

My dad's voice down the line was alien, so, so far away. 'Night, night, then, Katie love,' he said.

And Katie love said, 'Night, Dad,' and went back upstairs to bed.

Losing Sara always was, always had been, too awful a thing to happen. I couldn't let it happen, I couldn't let her go. So I clung on. Clung to her, clung to Glenn, clung to any old lies.

I could not let her go.

Sara came back alone, late. Glenn was sleeping but I'd stayed awake, listening for her. The back door slammed open and my heart started hammering. Sara crashed her way through the kitchen and up the stairs into her room. Beside me Glenn stirred.

'Ssh. It's Sara – I'll go,' I whispered and he fell back asleep.

I crept from the bed and waited a moment, just to be sure he stayed sleeping. My heart was racing but whatever happened if she was as drunk as she sounded she wouldn't remember anything anyway. I crept out on to the tiny landing and tapped on her door; quietly I opened it and went in just as she was falling back on to her bed. Her legs were bare; that's what I noticed first. She'd got on the rest of her clothes but her legs were still bare. I guess her tights were still tangled in the corner of that room somewhere, wherever they'd landed when *he'd* pulled them off; ripped now probably, not worth putting back on.

Her face was blanked out, whiter than white, make-up pretty well gone now apart from the black around her eyes and the red on her mouth, badly renewed at some point, chalk-thick and sliding, way off-centre. I thought she was unconscious but suddenly she sat up, said, 'Gotta pee,' and staggering badly she stood up, swaying on her bare feet as the pee ran down her legs and on to the floor, spreading out across the wood. Then as if she realized what she'd done she started crying, still with her eyes shut, and she sat back down on the bed again, head bowed into her hands, feet still in the wet.

I picked up a jumper from off the chair, threw it down on the floor and mopped it around with my foot. Sara just sat there, shivering from the cold and the drink, pink legs blotching white and blue.

I thought she might throw up. 'Are you going to be sick?' I barked at her like a school teacher. I put my arms on hers and shook her, gently at first, then harder, trying to rouse her. She rolled in my arms like a rag-doll.

'Go sleep,' she muttered, eyes shut, and toppled sideways, out of it.

I lifted her legs on to the bed but kept her on her side in case she *was* sick and choked. I didn't know what to do about her clothes; her skirt was wet and her knickers too if she was wearing any, but when I tried to lift her to undress her I couldn't, she was like a dead weight. So in the end I dragged the blankets over from the other bed and covered her with those, and got under them with her. Then I lay beside her with my arm around her middle, holding her so she was safe, holding her cold, clammy, filthy body into the warmth of mine, my legs curved into the back of hers, hand on her abdomen feeling it go in, out, in, out, just holding her.

I awoke in the morning still pressed against her, still holding her tight. She still slept; would do for a long time yet I guessed. She probably didn't even know I was there, but no matter. I had held her all night long. I moved my hand from her stomach, up over her body, and pushed the hair back from her neck. She didn't stir. I shifted up a bit so I could lean over her and see her face, squashed into the lipstick-stained pillow, mouth open, cracked and dry. I put my lips against her cheek and kissed her; still she did not stir, so I said what I wanted to say, what I'd wanted to say for weeks and weeks, since she'd first come to our school. I whispered it against her cheek so the words would stay, kissed into her skin. 'Sara, I love you.'

16

I went through a phase, when I was about nine or ten or so, of wishing myself disabled in some way, only the word I used was *special*.

First I pretended I had a bad leg. Whenever I went out, to the shops or to the park or wherever people were around to see me and pity me, I hobbled about like I was lame, dragging my weak leg behind me. Other times I pretended I was mute, and made up my own sign language which I tried out in sweet shops whenever I was away from Eppingham, pointing at what I wanted, waggling my fingers about and staring at the shopkeeper with big, doleful eyes.

All kids do this a bit, don't they? Make up their own languages and things, put on an act. But with me it was an obsession. I couldn't wait to escape into my fantasy life. At every opportunity I'd transform, from Kate the ordinary into Kate the mute, Kate the lame, Kate the special.

It was like an addiction, a total escape.

Then I met a blind girl, called Tanya. She was the daughter of some friends of my parents, and a couple of years older than me, which would have made her about eleven the first time we met. She had long, straight fair hair and the biggest blue eyes I'd ever seen. I thought she was really beautiful. She smiled a lot, which made her seem heroic and all the more tragic, and when she listened to people speaking she tilted her head in such a way that she seemed to be listening with her whole being. When we met she touched my face, running her hands over my nose, my cheeks, my jaw while I stared into her unseeing eyes, stricken. It seemed to me to be so desperately romantic then, to be blind, so I latched on to that as my new fantasy.

First I thought I would like to be blind from birth, like Tania, but then I realized that that would mean I wouldn't know what things looked like. No matter how much I touched and listened and brought to use all my other senses to help me I would never really *know*; I wouldn't know how a tree looked, or a house. All big things that couldn't be touched all over with my fingers would be forever unknown. Without experience even imagination is no good; I wouldn't even know what colour was and that was just unthinkable.

So I thought perhaps it would be better if I'd had some kind of accident that had left me blind. That way I'd still have the benefit of my previous sight. When meeting someone new I would be able to flutter my fingers over their features, concentrating, forming a picture in my mind, and I would be able to ask them

What colour are your eyes? And when they answered me *Blue* or *Brown* or whatever I would have their image, cast into my tragic, sightless mind.

But the trouble was I couldn't think of an accident that would take away my sight but leave the rest of me intact. So then I hit on the idea of an illness, and that opened a whole new passage to my fantasy. I pictured myself fading away against white linen sheets, a soft cooling breeze ruffling the half-drawn curtains of my sick-room window, my mother seated permanently by my bedside. I heard the quiet, stifled sobs, and felt the gentle hand on my brow, brushing back my hair. And that same hand holding a glass of water to my parched lips, helping me to drink. And in and out of the haze other people would come and go, always hushed, always weeping as they left.

And then we'd get the miraculous recovery, the answer to all those prayers; but the joy would be bittersweet because the illness had left me blind. Slowly but bravely I would have to find my way again, back into the world, using senses until now taken for granted. Tentatively reaching out with the help of those who loved me, gaining strength from their love, helped onwards by their prayers, made virtuous by my plight.

And so it went on, until I had all but convinced myself that I was Clara in the Heidi story.

I met Tania probably about five or six times in all. By

the time she was a teenager the pupils in her eyes had almost disappeared and her stare was no longer dreamy but turned inwards. She'd got greasy skin then, and greasy hair that needed to be washed every day and wasn't. And her clothes were awful, obviously chosen by her mother, who was too old and dead plain.

I felt sorry for Tania then, because she wasn't beautiful any more. And then I felt ashamed.

The thing is, there I was all those years ago wishing myself disabled in some way because I wanted to be special. I wanted the attention that being different would bring.

But now, suddenly, I realized I *was* different. And I hated it. I wanted to stop it, I wanted to hide it. I wanted it to just go away.

I *couldn't* be gay.

I thought of the weird guy who owned the hotel down by the river, and walked around Eppingham in his tight white trousers, wearing eyeliner. *He* was gay. We all loved to laugh at him.

We'd laugh at anything gay. We laughed at Toby because he wanted to play with the girls all the time, we laughed at Nathan because he signed his Christmas cards with 'love'. We laughed at Leone because she walked like a bloke and followed Amanda around like a lost dog. *Bender*, we'd say, laughing. *Bender*.

That's all it was; a laugh. Just kids having a laugh.

They wouldn't have known a real bender if they stared one in the face. They didn't see one when they looked at me. I didn't see one when I looked at myself in the mirror. I saw a kid like all the rest. Just a face, half-printed, still half-blank.

I thought of all the school discos that Juliet and I had been to – and we'd been to them all, showing off our clothes, our half-naked legs, our come-and-get-me hair. We were popular, Juliet and me, we danced with the boys. *I* danced with the boys. I put my hands around their necks and let them press their bodies against mine. I think of the last disco we went to, and I can't even remember who it was I got off with now, but I remember his spotty face and the smell of sweat from under his arms and how clumsily his hands groped their way up my back, trying to get to grips with my bra. I can't remember which boy it was, but I do remember that I put my head on his shoulder and turned my face away from his because there was no way, no way on earth, that I could bring myself to kiss him.

And I think of Juliet's party, and how it was decided beforehand that I would get off with Ed Stevens. I remember his hands rubbing up and down my back when I danced with him, and how I kept my face turned away from his. And I remember how glad I was that Juliet's family were in the next room, stopping anything from happening.

* * *

It isn't a black-and-white thing, it isn't definitive. It isn't like being blind, or mute. It's insidious. It creeps inside you slowly and it grows, so quietly it grows. So quietly, you could almost pretend it wasn't there.

On the Sunday after the party I stayed in my room pretty much all day, pretending I was doing homework, then that I was reading, then clearing out my old toy cupboard that Mum had been on at me to do for ages.

I sat on the floor among heaps of old books and games and boxes full of all sorts while the turmoil raged like an angry sea inside me. I tipped out the boxes, rummaged through heaps of dolls and plastic animals, trolls and little Disney characters, beads and bracelets and tiny sequined purses, the sort that you get in party bags, and miniature useful things from Christmas crackers: little brush and comb sets and mini sewing kits and tiny empty photo frames, treasures. I sorted these things into piles. Three piles, to be exact. One pile of things for charity, one of things for the bin and one of things to keep.

And as I worked I tried to do the same thing with my feelings; I tried to unwind the mess inside, and out from the confusion I pulled fear, disgust, and deep-down panic. I tried to separate these feelings, to locate the cause of each one. And I found there were three main things, three issues.

The first issue was plain enough: Sara was a tart. She must be. Only a tart would do what she'd been doing, at a party, with a bloke she hardly even knew. It made me so *mad* to think that she was a tart, but she was, she was. She *had* to be that she could just lie back, drunk, with her legs open with just anyone . . .

I started grabbing at my old dolls now, pulling at their arms and legs and their hair; it made me breathe so hard, this fury, it made me want to *hit* Sara because why did she have to be such a *tart*? I could feel myself starting to cry, with harsh tears that frightened me because they came from right down inside my heart where there was a dark, dark feeling that I didn't understand. I didn't understand it at all, so I came away from it, I came upwards, to what I did know, and that was issue two.

That I was *terrified* of losing her.

The other feeling, the other issue, the really *big* issue, the one that was causing all this turmoil in me in the first place, I ignored. I ignored the fact that I loved her, not as a friend, but really loved her, deep, deep down, like a comet, hurtling on and on, slamming through my world. More than Simon Leevy ever would with his cheap, grabbing hands, more than Andy ever did, *if* he did, more than any boy or man would because they only wanted one thing and I wanted all of her. This is what really mattered and I stuck it into the third pile marked *Invisible*, and blocked it out.

That is what you do when you treat feelings this way, as separate commodities to be pulled out and sorted. And that is what I did.

I stuck my emotions like old junk into neat, labelled piles.

17

I could not get it out of my mind, the image of Sara on that bed with Simon Leevy.

It stuck in my head, right at the front. On top of all the other pictures stored in there. Like a piece of film taped across my skull, just behind my eyes. Sara's pink-white skin and veiny legs, Sara's sweat and dirt and tangled hair, Sara's mouth, wide open, wet, screaming at me.

She wasn't going out with Simon now. She'd let him fuck her but she wasn't going out with him.

If she was, if it had been the burst of a new passion, if there was some kind of love in it somewhere, maybe I wouldn't have tortured myself so. I told myself that if Sara loved Simon I would accept it, I'd have to. I'd love her from the sidelines, like I was supposed to do, and everything would be fine. But she wasn't going out with him and I couldn't accept it. She'd let him fuck her but it meant nothing. She'd just given herself away, like *she* meant nothing.

That's the thing. I'd seen Sara, my precious Sara, opened up like a piece of meat for some nobody. I couldn't get it out of my head.

I wondered how much she even remembered, if she remembered any of it. It was hard to tell and I couldn't exactly ask her, could I? I couldn't say *Hey Sara, do you remember what happened at the party, how you were having it off with Simon Leevy and I walked in and saw?*

So I never mentioned it and she never mentioned it.

We saw Simon at school, of course. Sometimes we'd walk right past him; Sara ignored him and he ignored us. It doesn't take much to work out what he thought of her.

Though to my mind, he was no better. Indeed he was worse, much worse, for going at her like an animal like that.

Other people knew. It seemed to me like the whole world knew and the whole world was whispering. Someone else must have seen, or just guessed, and blabbed. Maybe Simon blabbed. Maybe he fucked her, told everyone, then ignored her.

Girls in Year Eleven gave Sara the dirtiest looks, and me too because I was with her. Girls in our year mostly gave Sara a bit of a wide berth anyway, but they talked about her, they bitched about her, and Melanie, who I hadn't spoken to for *months*, said to me one day in History, 'Why do you still go around with her, Kate? She's a dog.'

Sara had a hard shell and it seemed harder now. It closed around her like a shield. Beside her I felt shut out and feeble. I don't have a hard shell at all; I hated everyone staring, everyone talking.

Andy ignored us totally now, and Mark was never around any more. I'd see him in the playground sometimes with his black-eye healing up now and he'd say, 'All right, Kate?' if I walked right past him but that was all. And Glenn was mad at Sara because of Andy and Simon and all the things people were saying, so Sara was mad at Glenn for being mad at her.

It was awful. Everything had changed.

I kept crying, and that annoyed Sara. But I just couldn't help it. I'd try saying something to her about it all, like *I wish things were how they used to be*, and the words would wobble and I'd be crying again.

I knew I got on her nerves. But I couldn't stop it. I felt so out of sorts, had done for days. I knew I was losing Sara and I couldn't bear it, I couldn't let it happen so every day I'd see her, every day I'd try again to say something to reach over this great gap that seemed to have opened up between us.

'Sara, why don't you talk to me any more?'

We were sitting on a bench in the rec. It was only February but a beautiful spring-like day. Sara was eating an apple, a very bruised apple. She bit off the bad bits and spat them out hard so they landed with little pats on the gravel at our feet.

'Why don't you tell me things?' I could *hear* myself whining.

Sara closed her eyes, really slowly, and opened them again on a sigh as if to say *here we go again*. She took a last bite of her apple, flung the core and stared ahead, face set.

I hated myself but I had to go on. 'I mean, you just don't *talk* to me any more.'

'God, Kate, change the record, won't you?'

I could feel the tears pricking in my eyes; I couldn't stop them. She was just so *cold*.

'And don't start the waterworks again,' she muttered.

I pulled the cuffs of my cardigan down over my hands and wiped at my eyes. 'Sara, I just want to be your friend,' I sobbed.

'Then just get off my back.' She spoke slowly, through her teeth. 'I am just so sick of everyone on at me all the time.'

'I'm not everyone,' I sniffed. 'I'm your friend.'

'You nag me like a bloody old woman,' she said.

'I do not!' I pulled my hands away from my eyes, outraged.

'You do. All the bloody time. You're nagging me now.'

Sara stared at me, green eyes bright with anger. I stared back. Surely she must know I love her. Surely it was there in my eyes.

* * *

But I do not know what Sara saw when she looked at me.

She left me on the park bench, still crying. I suppose she went home, for what was left of lunchtime. When I left the rec and headed back to school I saw Glenn, coming up the other way, from their house.

'What's wrong?' he asked when he caught me up. 'What's happened with you and Sara?'

He looked at my eyes, which must have been red and bruised, and put his hands on my shoulders. Just this kindness made the tears start again and he pulled me against his chest. He smelt of their house; I sobbed into his jumper, breathing him in.

'Ssh,' he said. 'Ssh.'

The bell for school rang and I pulled myself away. It suddenly occurred to me that Sara would be coming along at any moment and I didn't want her seeing me like that now, with Glenn.

'Do you want to talk about it?' Glenn asked and I nodded.

'Yes,' I said. 'Later. Can I meet you after school?'

I met him outside the little post office at the far end of the High Street and we walked down to the river, where we went that time at Christmas. Sara wouldn't go there,

Sara wouldn't see us. We sat on the same bench, the one where we'd done it. Glenn put his arm around me and hugged me to him, as if remembering.

'It's Sara,' I said. 'She's really changed. She's in such a bad mood all the time but she won't tell me why. She won't *talk* to me.' I stopped for a moment, realizing I was firing off accusations, saying *she's* this, *she's* that.

'Is she upset about Simon Leevy?' Glenn asked.

'No it's not just that,' I said. 'She doesn't seem to *care* about that. No it's *me*. She's just being so off with me all the time and I don't know why.'

Glenn drew his arm away from my shoulder and got his fags out his jacket pocket. He took two out and stuck them both in his mouth to light them. 'She's got a lot on her plate at the moment,' he mumbled, cigarettes bobbing, and I wish I'd heeded him. I wish I'd said *What? Tell me*.

But I didn't. I just took my cigarette and said, 'Well she doesn't have to take it out on me.'

Glenn sighed, puffing out smoke. Eventually, reluctantly, he said, 'Do you want me to have a word with her?'

And I was so desperate to do anything to keep hold of her that I said yes.

The next morning I woke up feeling sick. I put it down to stress or exhaustion. I was so tired; my arms and legs felt as heavy as lead and I had to practically force myself out of bed. I went into the bathroom to get ready and splashed cold water on to my face. That made me feel a little better, but then I tried to clean my teeth; I squeezed the tube and out oozed the toothpaste on to the brush. It didn't smell right. I mean, it smelt pepperminty as usual but it was horrible; nausea stirred again in my stomach.

Maybe I was going down with something; that, or I'd eaten something dodgy.

I rammed the toothbrush inside my mouth, going straight for the back teeth as usual, and gagged. Every nerve in my mouth felt open and raw. I spat out the toothpaste, hung over the sink with my mouth open and my back teeth throbbing.

I would have stayed at home, only I had to go in; I had this stupid, ridiculous notion that everything would be fine today. That Glenn would have had his little word with Sara and everything would be rosy again.

How stupid can you be?

She ignored me in tutorial. She sat with her back turned to me, slouched over the desk, picking at a loose thread on her bag. And I sat beside her, pretending to read my French, with my teeth unclean and aching, and nausea rising through me in waves.

I wondered if Glenn had said anything to her yet. I wondered *what* he'd said to her.

227

I felt really sick, so I went straight up to the loos after tutorial to get a drink. I was bent over the water fountain when she came in behind me, slamming open the door and throwing her bag down so hard it skidded across the floor and hit my feet.

'I want a word with you,' she said and I stood up and wiped the water from my chin. 'What the hell do you think you're doing bitching to my own brother about me?'

She stood with her hands on her hips, body tilted forward and ready to fly, and spat the words out. Really spat, so that she had to wipe her mouth on her sleeve. I had never seen her so angry.

I grappled for words, and found none.

'What kind of a friend are you?' she went on. 'You're *no* friend. You think you can try and turn my own brother against me.'

'No I don't—'

'Taking him away from me wasn't enough for you, was it?' she shouted and her words echoed, bouncing off the stone walls. 'You've got to try and turn him against me now as well.'

'I haven't taken him away from you,' I said. 'And all I did was talk to him.' I put my hand over my nose and tried not to breathe; the smell of school toilets, of disinfectant and piss, was making me feel worse. 'I was worried about you—'

She snorted. 'Oh do me a favour. When did you ever think about anyone except yourself? You're just a user. That's what you are. A fucking user.'

'I am *not*!' I took my hand away then put it back again, swallowing, swallowing hard.

'Yes you are.' She looked like she was going to hit me. 'You used me to get my brother.'

'How can you *say* that?' It was so *unfair*. 'You set me up with him in the first place!'

'I don't remember you fighting him off.' She looked me up and down, like I was dirt, contempt all over her angry white face. 'And now you just follow me around all the time so you can see him.'

'I do not!' I could feel the bile rising in my throat, and my stomach tightening up. 'Sara, I want to be with *you*—'

'No you don't,' she sneered. 'You're just using me. But if you think you can turn my brother against me you can just forget it.'

'I'm going to be sick.' I clamped my hand over my mouth and my body heaved.

Sara stared at me in disgust. 'Good,' she said. 'I hope you choke on it.'

I went home after that. I had to; I'd got sick all down my top and my skirt. When my mum saw my miserable, red-eyed face she said, 'Poor you, was it something you ate, do you think?' and let me just lie on the sofa watching TV. I stared at the screen, not seeing anything, hurting all through my body, all through my head. How could Sara think that of me? How *could* she call me a user? She was so, so wrong.

How could she stand there and say those things and *hate* me, when I loved her so much?

I tried phoning her that evening. I dialled her number with my heart thumping and nerves jumping in my stomach, but I kept just getting a dead tone. So I called the operator, waited ages and ages to speak to someone, and when I finally got to ask what was wrong with Sara's phone the snooty woman on the line replied, 'I'm sorry. That number is no longer available.'

Next morning I woke up feeling sick again, but I had to go to school because I just *had* to speak to Sara and to Glenn. I had to put things right. I thought maybe I just felt sick because I was hungry as I didn't eat at all yesterday, so I had some toast and that did seem to help. I still couldn't clean my back teeth though; that was really weird.

But of course there was no point in speaking to Sara, not till she'd calmed down. I could tell that just by her face. She kept her expression mask-like, flat, and looked through me as though I just wasn't there.

So I hunted out Glenn, lured him away from Sara

again and made him be with me. I thought I'd have him on my side at least, but my, oh my, blood is thicker than water, that is what they say, isn't it? And of course their blood was not mine.

'What have you done to Sara?' Glenn asked as his fingers fiddled with my hair, pushing it back from my cheek.

'Nothing,' I said but my voice sounded lost, like I was talking through thick, thick wool. 'I haven't done anything. She just went mad at me.'

'Must be something,' he said and his finger was like a worm, weaving in and out of my hair. 'Some reason.'

'She said I used her to get to you.'

'Did you?' So softly he spoke and I could feel myself lulled, fooled.

'Of course not,' I said. '*She* was my friend first. She *wanted* me to get off with you! I only did it for her.'

He took away his finger, slowly. 'Oh thanks very much.'

'I didn't mean it like that.'

'Then how did you mean it?' he asked quietly, and I was floundering. I was losing. I was over a cliff edge, gripping on with oiled hands.

And still that sickness in my stomach kept on coming and going, slowing my thoughts and my responses, like a wound, holding me back.

'I don't want you upsetting Sara,' he said. 'She's got it hard enough already.'

* * *

It was like walking through a fog. I felt like I was wading through an endless blackness, pleading, pleading. Walking alone, up and down that road between their house and the school, waiting to see them, waiting to start it up again and say *You've got it all wrong*. Scribbling endless letters, the same words over and over, *Sara please, Sara please, please, please* . . . And all the time that constant sickness kept churning round and round in my body, so much there that I got used to it, I thought it must just be the pain.

18

'Got you some of these,' my mum said, unloading the shopping from bags, and she tossed a box of tampons at me. I caught the box and held it to my chest.

My mum shops late on Friday afternoons. On that afternoon it was raining; she'd got wet just bringing the bags in from the car. Raindrops clung to her hair and sparkled like diamonds, glittering as she moved.

'You'll be needing them soon. Same time as me, aren't you, usually?' She stopped what she was doing, smiled at me sympathetically, woman to woman. 'Next week then I suppose.'

Up in my room I opened my dressing table drawer and there among my other bits and pieces were three more boxes of tampons, unopened. I stared at them while my heart beat a hard heavy *thud*, *thud*, *thud* and my face and my eyes started to burn.

I slammed the drawer shut quick, suddenly terrified my mum might come in, but I could hear her still down in the kitchen, getting things ready for supper. So I opened the drawer again, tore open one of the boxes and pulled out a handful of tampons, then stuffed them and one of the unopened boxes into my school bag, for now, for somewhere to put them, until I could take them to school tomorrow and throw them away.

I tried to remember my last period and couldn't. Not since Christmas. *Before* Christmas. How many was that missed then? Three? Two? Or just one missed and another one very, very late? I couldn't think. Was it every four weeks or every calendar month? I was never that regular anyway, and I never kept note or anything, so maybe . . .

I sat down on my bed, heart and mind racing.

I mean, just nerves could make it late, couldn't they?

I thought back to Glenn and me, thought back over the times we'd done it. He kept a packet of condoms in the drawer by his bed and mostly he used one, except once or twice maybe, like the first time and that time after the party, and that time by the river . . . Oh I don't know, it could have happened any of those times, but I swear to God I thought if you were careful most of the time you'd be OK.

Now and again wouldn't hurt.

Oh God, I swear I really believed this.

Now and again wouldn't get you pregnant. Not if you were careful most of the time. And not if you were like *me*. Girls like me didn't get pregnant. Stupid girls got pregnant; thick girls.

Slags got pregnant.

* * *

Into the next week I waited, suspended, while the sickness came and went in waves and my back teeth remained unclean. My mum said we'd be on next week, so on I prayed I would be. But next week came and nothing with it. I took tampons from my drawer each day: I took them to school and threw them away, unopened. I sat at my desk in stuffy classrooms and moved on my chair, imagining I could feel something at last and then I'd rush to the loo at break, but still nothing. I *willed* myself into stomach aches, thinking at every second of every day that this was it, this had to be it . . .

But nothing. Nothing at all.

'I got us a treat,' my mum said on Wednesday when she came in from work. 'Thought we needed it.'

She unwrapped a chocolate cake, a fresh one, from the baker's in the village. And I had to sit at the table with her and gorge on chocolate because that is what we crave, that is what we need, us women, if we are lucky enough to get our period.

And Sara's silences, Sara's flinging down her bag, flinging down herself at her desk, and all her huffing and flouncing about meant nothing now. I was on a different plane, like reality had shifted, and I had slipped, right out the door.

Day in, day out, I moved as usual and did all the usual things, but I could think of nothing but the secret rooted in my body and do nothing but wait to see if it would disappear like a dream on a tampon.

19

I told Sara I was late. That's how I put it: *Sara, I'm late.*
It seemed to have some film star quality about it. It
seemed *romantic*.

I'd written her a note saying *There's something I have to
tell you, something awful . . .* And she came. Out of
curiosity I suppose, if nothing else.

I sat on the bench and drew hard on my cigarette,
and I told her.

'What do you mean *late*?' She sat back away from me,
horror all over her face.

'Well . . . you know . . .' I flicked the hand that held
the cigarette, gesturing to the world.

'No I don't know.' She jumped up and stood facing
me. She waved her arms about as she said, 'Days late?
Weeks late? What do you mean, exactly? Have you done
a test?'

'Well, no . . .'

'Then do one for God's sake! Don't go round saying
you're pregnant when you might not be. Do a bloody test!'
Then she sat down again, and rummaged in her bag for
her fags. 'But tell me the results for God's sake, won't you?'

And I took that as a sign that she cared.

237

* * *

There was no way I could go into the chemist in Eppingham and say *Can I have a pregnancy test please?* so the next day I caught the bus to Lewiston after school, on my own. I'd hoped Sara might come with me. She hadn't spoken to me all day again but several times she'd caught my eye, stared hard for emphasis and mouthed the words *Do it*.

She didn't come with me, though. She waited for me by the school gates and walked with me to the bus stop, walking just behind me, not talking to me. And at the bus stop she stood well away from me, as if she couldn't bear to be near me. When the bus came she hung around just long enough to make sure I actually got on it and got my ticket, then she was gone, marching up the road with her head down and her hands stuffed into the pockets of her jacket. I took my ticket and my change from the driver and I turned and watched her go; she didn't even look up as the bus pulled away and passed right by her.

The front half of the bus was full of standing kids, squashed up against each other and swaying about, arms upstretched, holding on to the bars. I pushed my way through them and sat at the back, right where Sara and I had sat that time when we went shopping after school, ages and ages ago. I tortured myself with the contrast, with the empty space beside me, missing her, missing *us*, the way we used to be. In my mind I conjured up her face, her smile, and I went over and over the things we said that time, just to get her voice inside my head again, to hear it before it became laden with hate.

The bus ride was making me feel sick again, compounding my misery. I tried to open the air vent above the window but it was stuck; I pushed hard at it but just the effort made me feel worse and I had to sit back down again, quick, breathing hard to steady my stomach. I sat in the other seat this time, Sara's one, and turned my body to the window and stared out; I stared at the houses and the cars and all the greyness of the damp and drab street but mostly I stared at my face, reflected back at me in the glass, ghostly white and miserable.

The bus rolled and lurched and my insides did the same. I put my forehead against the window but the bus jolted and I banged my head on the glass. I really wanted to get off but we were still a long way out of Lewiston, too far to walk. I thought if I could just hold on a bit longer . . . The bell rang for the next stop and loads of people got off then so the bus was still for quite a while and I felt a little better. I'd make it to the next stop, at least, maybe the one after. It was a long, long road between Eppingham and Lewiston and the bus stops were spread far apart, but there were fewer people on the bus now and it didn't even stop at the next two stops, it just hurtled on by, which was fine. I thought I'd be OK if it kept moving at a steady pace. But just before the next stop someone pressed the bell at the last minute, for a laugh, no doubt, to make the driver slam on his breaks, which he did, and the bus skidded and jerked to a halt. The few kids left at the front swung from their bars like monkeys, banging into each other and screeching with laughter, and I was thrown right forward, out of my seat. I shot my hands out to save myself, clutched on to the rail across the top of the seat in front, and threw up.

It spattered as it hit the floor. I managed to turn my head sideways, just in time so that it didn't go on my skirt, but it splashed all over my shoes and on my legs. And there was more coming. I had some tissues in my bag, one of those little handy packs; I reached sideways, fumbling inside my bag for them and the second lot came, splattering on the floor. I kept my head right over this time, and stayed like that, catching my breath, while I got those tissues out and wiped the sick off my face. It was all over the floor; I didn't know what to do. The bus started up again and it spread sideways into a stream, running under the seats towards the front. I threw the tissue that I'd wiped my face with on to the floor, stopping the flow. There weren't many tissues in the packet and I didn't want to use them all but I took out another, separated the two sheets and dropped them down like parachutes, over the worst of the mess. Still bending down, I gathered up my bag and stepped over the sick, into the aisle, pressed the nearest stop bell and stood, holding on to a pole, till we reached the next stop.

Amazingly, no one seemed to have noticed, even though it stank. I think they were too busy having their own party up the front to even realize that I was there. Out of the corner of my eye I watched new streams running out from under that tissue covering, creeping towards people's shoes and bags, and as soon as the bus stopped and the doors hissed open I was off, before anyone else.

The river ran parallel to the road into Lewiston, and just a little further along from the bus stop there was a gap between the houses, and some steps leading down to the open space by the river bank. This was paved over mostly, with little square patches of garden going down in steps, like a terrace. Nothing grew in these gardens, not at this time of year, they were just mud patches, piled up with dog shit in various stages of decay. There were several benches, all facing the river, and all covered in grafitti. I ran down the steps and sat on the nearest one, next to one of the gardens, but the smell of dog shit was so rank that I had to move to another.

There was no one else around except a woman with a pushchair loaded up with shopping and a small child on reins, down near the water's edge. They were having a fight, this woman and child, over a bag of bread.

'Give it to the ducks,' the woman shouted. 'Give it to the ducks.'

'No,' the kid shouted back. 'Won't.'

The child held on to the plastic bag with both hands, clutching it to his chest. He glared at his mother. His mother glared back.

'Give it to the bloody ducks,' mother yelled, and stamped her foot.

'No!' The kid stamped his foot too, then the other foot, and so on, till he was jumping on the spot.

The woman tried to grab the bread and the kid flung it, bag and all, into the river.

'Now look what you've done!' mother screeched and she smacked the child, hard, across his backside. He started screaming and the sound split through the air at such a pitch that I wanted to cover my ears. The woman forced him into the pushchair, pressing his rigid little body in the middle to hold him down while he screamed and screamed, then they headed off, leaving the ducks to choke on the plastic.

I sat there till the screaming faded out of earshot, lost in the general hum of traffic on the road up behind me. Then I took the remaining tissues out of my bag, spat on one to wet it, and tried to wipe the sick off my shoes and tights. It came off my shoes OK, except for around the edges where it had gone right into the stitching, but I didn't care too much about that. I couldn't get it off my tights, though. I wore thick, black opaque tights, and the tissue broke up as I rubbed at them, leaving little bits stuck in the material. I rubbed and rubbed and made it worse, till I gave up and started walking the rest of the way into Lewiston, with sick and wet tissue ground into my woolly legs.

I was terrified of bumping into someone I knew, and of them seeing what I was buying, so I had to find a chemist right out of the way where no one from school or from Eppingham would possibly walk in. So I walked right down the High Street, past all the shops and the precinct, and under the railway bridge and out towards the police station. There was a fishmonger's just under the railway bridge, one that opened out on to the road. The smell of it made me gag again and I had to hold my breath till my ears popped, and not breathe at all until I was way past.

I knew there'd be a chemist somewhere along that road. Past the dry cleaner's and the charity shops and the pizza take-aways. I vaguely remembered seeing one once from the car.

When I found it there was just the chemist himself in there in his white coat, standing behind the counter. The bell above the door rang as I pushed it open and he looked up, peering at me over his glasses. I walked past the shelves, slowly, trying to find what I needed and I could feel him watching me. I expect he thought I was a shoplifter. He'd be right of course but today I was worse than that. Today I was a pregnant teenager, a silly little tart; *that* is what I saw on his face when I found the boxes at last, on the main counter right under his nose and said, 'Can I have one of these, please?'

I stuffed it into my bag and got back out into the street again as fast as I could and hurried back into the town centre to get the bus home. I felt like everyone was looking at me, damning me; old ladies and mothers with small children, all looking at me and labelling me with their eyes. When the bus came I got on and went straight to the back and sat with my bag shut tight on my lap. It was worse than having a stolen shirt in there, much worse.

I couldn't believe I was doing this. It was all so unreal.

When I got home I took my school bag upstairs to my room, closed the door and took out the pregnancy kit, still inside its paper bag. It was a white bag, sterile and clean, with just a green cross and the address of the chemist's printed on one side. The paper crackled as I unwrapped it, like a Christmas gift, like sweets, like a nice surprise. I thought the box would be heavier, as it was supposed to have a whole kit inside. I thought of all the other kits I'd bought in the past; the badge-making kits, kits to sew your own glove-puppets, the grow-your-own-garden-in-a-box kit I got my dad for his birthday once, years ago. Kits full of all sorts of weird bits and pieces, all vital for making something out of nothing. But this kit wasn't heavy. This kit was so light it could be empty; I closed my eyes and imagined it was a baker's box in my hand. Inside was just one fluffy-light eclair, that was all.

But this kit wasn't for the making of something out of nothing, and there would be no nice surprise inside. This kit was just a word; a yes or a no. It was the judge when he put his black hat on and banged down his hammer; it was the examiner who knew you had cheated all year long; it was a puff of God.

On the outside of this lightweight box of heaven and hell and nothingness was a blued-out photograph of a woman. It's funny, I felt like I'd seen that woman before. And then I realized that I had, her or someone very much like her, in the classified sections in magazines like *Company* and *Cosmopolitan*. She always had the words *Pregnant? There is one way to be sure* or *Abortion: phone blah, blah, blah* written underneath her. I'd seen her, but I'd never thought I'd ever need to take any notice of her. Now, looking at her, I wondered why they'd blocked her out in blue. Was a blue woman more appropriate somehow than a real, live, full-colour one? She had brown hair, really, this woman, I just knew she did, sleek and shiny. It fell slightly over her face, which was in profile, looking downwards, meek and somewhat pensive. She looked serene, and so, so, sophisticated. You could just tell there'd be a rich man somewhere in the background waiting for the good news. They'd captured it all in this photograph and then they'd blued it out.

Even the abortion ads were elevated by this woman. She wasn't just a fifteen-year-old tart, banged up, equating pregnancy kits to chocolate cakes in boxes.

My parents were downstairs in the kitchen, safely out of the way. I opened this little box of tricks and found inside a plastic moulded tray containing two lolly sticks and a booklet of instructions. Piss on the stick, it said, though it caged it nicely. Piss on the stick and watch magic turn it blue.

I tucked the kit in the second drawer of my bedside table, underneath my knickers and socks. I'd read the instructions, I knew what to do. I tucked it there carefully, and later, when I went up to bed, I opened the drawer and took one little peep. I peeled the socks away from her face like reeds away from a corpse and there she was, the ghost in my drawer. I tried to picture her pissing on a stick but I couldn't.

I lay in my bed and I had this feeling that I was like a sentence about to be said, like in a play; I was the next line. Not there until spoken; anticipated, oh yes, but not there. Not yet. I was that dead moment between breaths; you breathe in, you breathe out, *you pause*, you breathe in again. That was me, that pause. That is how I felt, then; I was neither one thing nor the other, I was the bit in the middle; suspended.

And in the morning I hid the kit under my bathrobe and sneaked it into the bathroom. Then I peed onto the stick and I waited, and I watched as the blue line appeared.

I pictured it, growing inside my skinny body.

I sat on the edge of the bath in my pyjamas, holding the blue-striped lolly stick in my hand, and my mind raced ahead like a wild thing unleashed. I pictured their baby, tiny and whole inside me, like Thumbelina. *Their* baby. I pictured it with bright green eyes and red-blonde hair. A girl, of course, it would have to be a girl. A girl just like Sara, *my* Sara, mine to hold and love and own. And I'd call her Sara, but with an *h* on the end, *Sarah*, to differentiate. I'd marry Glenn of course, and I'd live in their house, with them and my baby; *our* baby.

That is what I was thinking on the inside, that is what whirled out from my heart and my soul while on the outside I was terrified; on the outside, across my shoulders, my back, all over my skin fear broke out like the cold in goosebumps.

I walked to school with their baby inside me, and I walked carefully, steadily, not too fast. I was afraid to move too fast. I was afraid it might fall out, whole, on to the street. I was afraid that it was in there, inside me. I was afraid mostly of course because I was only fifteen and I was pregnant, but oh God, there was this elation whipping up through me, half-nightmare, half-dream.

This was what I wanted, wasn't it? Though I'd never actually *thought* of it, never dreamt of it. This was what I'd wanted down, down in my heart. This was the life that would bind us; we were as one now, we three. We were joined, forever.

Sara could not turn away from me now. We were in this together.

I had her brother's baby, here in my body. I touched my hand across my stomach, warm. His baby, their baby, her baby, here in my body.

We were bound, now. She could not shut me out.

20

I'd put the lolly stick in my bag, to show her. Somehow I knew I'd need it. I knew I'd need proof.

Sara said, 'You're making this up. You're fucking making this up.'

But I had the lolly stick; I had the proof. The blue line was a little smudged now from being in my bag but it was still there, still very definitely there.

We were in the rec, by the Scout hut. The nearest place to the school that we could go to and talk in private. It was a bright, windy day; Sara's hair whipped across her face and into her eyes as she stared down at the stick in my hand, then up at my face in horror.

'I don't fucking believe it,' she said, but she did of course. She had to, now she'd seen the proof.

'I mean, what the fuck did you think you were *doing?*' She pushed her hair off her face with her hand but the wind blew it straight back again; thick copper strands beating at her skin. She glared at me, with the hair flipping in and out of her eyes, glared as if she could intimidate me out of this. As if I'd give in under her stare and take it all back, and say *It was a mistake, I'm not pregnant after all, I didn't mean it.*

I said nothing. Under the pressure of my fingers the lolly stick snapped in half, sharp. Oh did I ever have such stupid ideas of saying *Sara it's your little niece in here: it's yours as much as mine, we'll share it. We'll love it together.*

She waved her hands in front of her, fingers stretched out in anger, slicing at the air. 'Didn't you use anything? Are you *stupid*? Did you do it deliberately? Did you think you could trap him?'

She said everything horrible she could think of. She even said, 'Maybe it's not Glenn's anyway. Maybe it's some other bloke's. You slept with Glenn quick enough, I'm sure you'd sleep with anyone.'

And then she said, cold as cold with the wind driving false tears into her winter eyes, 'You'll have to get rid of it.'

I did not reckon on this, not for a moment. In a day I'd had a million dreams. I'd got my life painted out in rosey hues. Of course I knew it would be difficult, having a baby at my age. Of course I knew there'd be shock, disapproval, anger to deal with – though not from *Sara*. In my madness I hadn't expected it from Sara. I'd expected capitulation, love; this life would unite us.

This life.

'What do you mean, get rid of it?' The wind whipped the words from my mouth and echoed them back at me.

Sara rolled her eyes as if she found me just too dense

for words. 'Get an *abortion*.' She laid on the emphasis, like I was thick, like I needed the word ramming home.

'I'm not having an abortion.' I said it so calmly, so flat. Sara's eyes glinted, stoking up for a fight.

'Yes you fucking are,' she said.

She stared at me, I stared at her.

'I am not having an abortion,' I said again and something inside me lifted to a different place, removed from ground level. Beyond all this . . . *dirt*.

If ever I was Sara's puppet those strings were now cut, well and truly.

'I am not getting rid of my baby.' Never, never in a million years. For all my conviction my voice was starting to shake now. 'It's Glenn's baby too. How do you think he'd feel if I just went and got an abortion?'

'Don't you even fucking tell him,' she spat at me. 'Don't tell anyone. Don't you *dare* mess up my brother's life. This is *your* problem. You just get yourself an abortion. *Do it*. Just get yourself an abortion and then just fuck off, out of our lives.'

She pushed me, not hard, but I stepped back and knocked into the Scout hut behind me. She wanted to slap me, to tear out my hair, to scratch out my eyes; I could see by the way she was shaking that she wanted to rip me to pieces. But she didn't; no one hits a pregnant woman. She killed me with her eyes then flung around and stormed off, fast, across the field.

* * *

Glenn cried when I told him.

We were down by the river, sitting on that same bench. Someone had carved *Vince and Cathy forever* into the wood; we sat either side of this promise and I ran my finger up and down the V, up and down. It must have been a regular little hot spot, that bench. You could tell that just from the amount of fag butts scattered on the asphalt around our feet. I wondered how many babies had been conceived there, down on that dirt.

Glenn sat with his elbows on his knees and his head in his hands and his fingers pushed up into his hair, and he cried. *I* felt sorry for *him* but I didn't know what to say. The words we needed were *It'll be all right* but it wasn't for *me* to say them; they needed to come from him. So I just sat beside him on the bench, running my finger up and down that V, and I looked at him. I looked at the curve of his back and his shoulders, shaking slightly as he cried, and at the shape of his head, cradled in his hands. I thought of his bed and the warmth of his body under the sheets and the smell of his pillow. I thought of the closeness. Sitting there with the cold wind coming off the river and blowing at my face and my hair I really *ached* for that closeness.

Tentatively I lifted my hand and put it on his back, and I started to move a little closer but he looked up suddenly, staring at the river with his wet eyes. And then he stood up, away from me.

'Look, I can't think now,' he said. 'We'll talk tomorrow.'

Three days in a row we met after school and walked down to the river. Wednesday, Thursday, Friday. Three days, because that is how long it took for him to get it sorted in his head.

Wednesday he just cried. Thursday he stared at me hard, saying, 'Are you sure? I mean, are you *positive*? It could be a mistake, couldn't it, just a scare?' Over and over he said this. Over and over as if repetition would make a difference, as if I could possibly change my mind. But by Friday he'd got it all sorted.

On Friday he said, 'I'll pay, of course.'

And it flashed through my head, that tone of voice, that noble offer, but those were not the right words. *I'll marry you, of course* was what he meant to say.

'For the abortion,' he said, for I must have looked blank, *stunned*.

Then he turned back to his fag, took a long drag and waggled the butt between his fingers. 'Don't know where I'll get the money from, though.'

And that's what mattered, wasn't it? That was the important thing. Where would the two hundred pounds or whatever was needed to pay for my baby to be killed come from? But no matter, Glenn would find it. Glenn would do the right thing.

Was I supposed to say *thank you*? Was I supposed to be *relieved*?

Suddenly all I could do was laugh. It was all so ridiculous, so hideously unreal that I had to laugh. If I'd kept the hundred and fifty pounds or whatever it was that I gave to Sara that time I could have paid for it myself! It was just all too much and I laughed and laughed, and Glenn stared at me, shocked.

It was macabre, that's what it was.

Then suddenly I wasn't laughing any more. I was crying. Hard, hard crying with my mouth still open on a laugh and I couldn't stop myself. I couldn't stop the awful wail that was coming up from deep down inside. I could not stop the tears.

Now Glenn was embarrassed, I'm sure he was. This whole performance was probably more than he ever expected to encounter on any one day. His cheeks coloured; he squirmed uncomfortably.

But he did the right thing. Let it always be said that Glenn did the right thing.

He patted my shoulder, gave it a rub.

'Don't worry,' he said. 'It'll be all right.'

I lay on my bed, naked, and splayed my hands over my stomach. I pressed gently, very gently, with my fingertips, to see if I could feel it.

I'd cried so much that the pillow was wet and cold beside my ears and my face was sticky. I thought of it like an insect, under my hands. I thought how easily I could crush it with my fingers. If I pressed hard enough I could kill it myself.

I didn't of course; I couldn't. I couldn't even feel it in there.

I thought of Gin bottles and knitting needles and all those horrible stories of how to kill a baby, and I cupped my hands over where it must be, cradling it deep inside me.

This unwanted child of theirs.

He got the money. He got the two hundred pounds that he thought was needed and pulled it out of his jacket pocket in screwed-up tenners. His fingers shook as he tried to give it all to me.

We were standing in the street not far from school; people were all around us, school kids going home. We stood to one side, on the pavement. Sara was a little further down the road, watching us; obviously she couldn't bear to be any nearer to me than that. They were waiting for me when I came out of school, could not wait even to get to somewhere more private, somewhere more appropriate for this sordid deal.

They just wanted it over with.

'I don't want your money,' I said to Glenn, but still he held it out to me in his nervous, trembling hands.

'Go on,' he said, pushing it at me, but I kept my hands down by my sides. 'There's two hundred quid. It should be enough.' And my, my, hadn't he done his homework, because next he said, 'And I've got a number you can ring. I've written it down.'

I said nothing; I couldn't. There was a lump in my throat hard enough to choke me and it took all my will to keep the tears from coming up. I stared at his hands, pushing that money at me, and saw that his wrists and the backs of his hands were red as if from a rash. I looked up, and saw that the colour began right up on his ears and spread down his neck and under the collar of his shirt. I pictured his body, flushed under his clothes. Flushed like it was when he fucked me.

'There's a place you can go. In North Shere. I've got the address.'

Why thank you, I supposed I should say. *How thoughtful.* Did they really expect me to take their money and take the address and trot straight off to kill my baby? *Their* baby?

'I've written it down.' He started to dip back into his pocket but that money was a bit cumbersome. That money needed holding on to with two hands. 'Here,' he said and tried to shove it at me again. 'Take this and I'll give it to you.'

I wouldn't take it. I shook my head hard and for all my effort the tears spilt out and started rolling down my cheeks.

Now he was floundering, now he was really nervous. And he didn't know what to do with that money. He fingered it like he was counting it in his head, checking it was all there. Eventually he put it back in his pocket, and said, 'Look, I've got it here then, OK?'

I blinked hard and looked past him, and saw Sara throw out her arms in a gesture of frustration. It must have been killing her to have to watch all this from a distance. It must have killed her to see that money go back in Glenn's pocket.

Now that his hands were free Glenn didn't know what to do with them; he pushed them through his hair; he held them out as if he might touch me. He sighed, he hesitated. I stood there crying and eventually he *did* touch me; he put his hands on my arms to comfort me. 'Look,' he said, and he must have *dreaded* it coming to this. 'I'll come with you if you want.'

And my, oh my, wasn't that just the last word in chivalry?

I would rather have died myself than kill my baby.

Suddenly I just wanted to get away from them both, right away. I couldn't bear Glenn touching me. I shook off his arms, pushing them away with my own hands, and stepped back, away from him. That was too much for Sara. She started running up the street towards us, her breath coming cloudy into the damp air.

'What's she doing?' She stared at me but it was Glenn she was talking to. 'What's going on? Why didn't she take the money?'

I couldn't speak for crying or I'd have answered her myself. I'd have said *Keep your money, I don't need it!*

'I don't know,' Glenn said, well out of his depth now the histrionics were flowing free. 'She doesn't want it.'

'Doesn't want it!' Sara screeched. 'What do you mean she doesn't want it?' She rounded on me like an animal, like a cat, ready to leap. 'What's the matter with you?' No one was around now and her voice echoed down the street. 'Are you fucking mad?'

'For God's sake, Sara,' Glenn said in a sort of stage whisper, glancing around him, obviously terrified that people were going to start creeping out from the houses, and the alleyways, and the shadows down the street; an audience, witness to this awful scene. 'Calm down, will you—'

'*Me* calm down?' Sara shrieked. 'Don't tell *me* to calm down. She's the one that's fucking mad!'

She pushed me; Glenn grabbed her arms, holding her back. 'Sara, leave it,' he said.

I turned to get away; I wanted to run away as far as I could from both of them but Sara broke free from Glenn and grabbed at me again, screaming, 'Don't you fucking turn away from me!' Then to Glenn she yelled, 'Give me the money. Give me the fucking money.' And like her puppy he started rummaging in his pocket and she snatched the ten-pound notes as he got them out. They fluttered about as she grabbed at them; she clamped them tight into her fists and rammed them at me. 'Here. You take it,' she screamed at me. 'This is our fucking food for a month. This is our fucking gas bill. This is our fucking rent, you conniving prick-teasing little whore.'

She pushed the money into my chest, but I wouldn't take it so she pulled back a second and then slammed it into my stomach, into our baby. I doubled over, winded, as the notes drifted to the ground.

'Sara!' Glenn lunged between us and pulled Sara away. He held on to her while she fought against him, trying to break free. Looking down as I was now, with my body bent over and my arms clutched around my middle, I watched their shoes trampling ten-pound notes into the damp and gritty pavement.

'Get off me!' Sara screeched at Glenn. 'Just fucking get off me. What are you taking her side for anyway? She's fucking ruined you! And if she won't get an abortion I'll do it for her.'

Did I plan it? Did I? Could I have done, on some deep, deep level? Could I have planned it all, deliberately?

I staggered home, still crying, still bent over a bit at first until I realized I could stand up straight and walk normally. She hadn't really hurt me. By the time I was out on the main street I was walking like nothing had happened. I'd even got my face back into shape for the benefit of passers-by. It's amazing what you can do, it's amazing how you can act when you have to, and I had to; I couldn't take my hysteria home with me.

But this doubt settled on me and stuck. Had I planned it? Had I, on some subconscious level?

I wanted their baby. I knew that from the minute I saw that lolly stick turn blue. But had I actually planned it, and meant to get myself pregnant? Was I all those things that Sara accused me of?

Was it a case of if I couldn't have Sara, I'd have her brother's baby instead?

21

I put on weight straight away. Not much really but on my skinny body every pound stood out like pantomime padding, on my breasts, my hips, my middle. It happened so quickly, fat stuffing out my skin. Every morning and every night I stood naked in front of my mirror, studying the change. If I stood up close I could just see myself from the rib cage upwards with my swollen breasts forcing my nipples out proud and pointed like mini traffic cones. But if I stepped back I could see more of me, all of me, down as far as my knees. And I did step back and I did stare – I'd never taken much notice of my body but now I recognized it not one little dot as mine. I stared at my stomach, expecting to see it swell in front of my eyes, full up, round, ready to burst. I puffed it out, I pulled it in again. It wobbled slightly, very slightly, fat under the skin now where there used to be none.

I started wearing the button on my school skirt undone and the zip half-down and I pulled my jumper down over the waistband to hide it. And I switched back to jumpers instead of cardies to hide my polo top because that strained now, over my chest. I wore the jumper big, so it would hide me. In my line of vision I could see my breasts now, like a constant shadow, always there, like the tip of my nose.

My breasts *hurt*. I couldn't do PE any more. I couldn't run at all without my breasts *killing* me. So I started making excuses; I started forgetting my kit, getting a headache, having my period (oh joke of jokes!) and if that didn't get me out of it I just plodded along slow behind everyone else, useless.

I thought our PE teacher might have guessed what was wrong with me. She looked at me with shrewd eyes and I was terrified she was going to say something to me. Maybe she would have done, in another week or two, if she'd had the chance.

In lessons I kept my head down, so I at least looked as if I was working. And from class to class I'd walk with my bag clutched in front of me, hiding my body, and at break I just walked about, trying to look as if I was going somewhere, or I hung about in the corridors, sorting out my bag, looking for something, being busy. I avoided everyone.

Incredibly, my parents didn't notice. I put on a good act; I came and went as usual, I hid myself in my room. I fooled them well.

They noticed that I wasn't seeing Sara any more, though. Noticed that I wasn't going round her house, and that I didn't talk about her any more. They didn't say anything, but they noticed all right. Saturday nights at home they fairly doted on me: *What do you fancy for supper, Kate? What DVD would you like to see tonight, Kate?* They must have thought that little chat we'd had after Christmas had done the trick at last, that I'd finally seen sense.

They must have just been so *pleased* that I wasn't seeing Sara any more that they just didn't notice anything else.

My mum and dad have photos of me as a baby, loads of them, dotted about the house. The best ones are in albums, stacked in the bureau in the living room, and duplicates of these peep out from shelves and drawer tops and windowsills all over the house. All different sizes and in all sorts of frames. Some are the usual instant-camera family shots but mostly they are studio shots, black-and-white, staged, perfect.

My dad's best friend was a photographer. He emigrated to America years ago, but before he went he took all these photos, millions of them, of black-haired, black-eyed little me, dressed up in a little white dress and playing, *preening*, under the lights.

And my mum and dad kept them all. I suppose that is how you feel when you have a baby, just one baby. You cannot see enough of it. You want it everywhere, all around you.

* * *

I never thought my baby might have dark brown eyes and dark brown hair, like me. I never thought it might look like me, like those pictures of me, scattered about its grandparents' house.

Sara was waiting for me in the corridor after English. As soon as the lesson had finished she'd got out the class quick then she stood to one side, waiting, while everyone else piled out.

And I knew it was absurd but the sight of her waiting for me still shot up spores of hope, unstoppable hope inside me. I saw Sara's body turned towards me, Sara's eyes, seeking out, holding mine. *This* time I might say sorry and she would hear me, she would forgive me, she would say *I know; me too.*

The thing is, when you love someone the way I loved Sara, love them as if it was always in you, part of your very being, its end is drawn out of you like an endless slow bleed and any attention is an ease to the pain. Any attention at all.

'Well?' she said, and how is it that one word can be so loaded?

Well, have you killed that baby yet? Well, when are you going to? Well, have you fixed it up? Well? Well?

She stared hard at me, beautiful eyes framed with furry black mascara.

'Well what?' I said like the slow one, and anger brightened her eyes, burning amber into green, like a marble warmed in the hand.

'You do it.' She spoke quietly but I heard her clearly enough, never mind that pushing past us were a hundred other people, shoes clattering, voices loud, pitched and shrill. 'You do it,' she said and I heard all the threat in her words. 'And you do it soon.' Then for good measure, just in case I hadn't got the message yet, she added, 'And stay away from my brother.'

She stepped back then, and looked me up and down, slowly. Then she flung her bag up on to her shoulder and turned to walk away, but before she did she said. 'D'you know what you look like? Do you know what you look like now?' Satisfaction smirked across her face. 'You look like a stupid fat *tart*.'

Those were her words. I remember them well. Those were Sara's last words to me.

Imagine it, a little baby unwanted. Suddenly they were everywhere, on TV between the programmes, on envelopes that came through the door. Faces of poor children, hungry children, suffering children, unloved children. It killed me over and over. Even nature programmes were full of it, full of pain and birth and throw-away life. I couldn't bear it. I couldn't bear to see those babies, human babies, animal babies, any babies. Couldn't bear to see them so unwanted.

Oh God, imagine it, inside me, in my body, my poor, poor dear unwanted baby.

22

I'd stopped feeling sick but then it came back, sudden, even worse than before. We were in March now, still winter in theory, and the heating was on full pelt at school but outside the weather had turned muggy and warm. It had rained for days, on and off, that annoying drizzly rain that weighs down on you and drives into your face and gets you soaked. I wished it would rain properly; I wished it wouldn't rain at all. I couldn't seem to breathe. There didn't seem to be any *air*. Outside you were hot in your coat, but you had to wear it else you'd get drenched, and inside you were hot because the heating was turned up so high.

The radiators ran along the outside wall of the classroom, underneath great high windows that only opened at the top. Thick old industrial radiators, pumping out their heat. The Maths classroom was on the first floor, overlooking the playing fields, but you couldn't see them, you couldn't see anything out those windows because the glass was all steamed up and where the steam ended there was just the endless nothingness of the grey, wet sky.

I took off my jumper. I had to. I eased my arms out

first then pulled it forwards over my head, trying to keep my polo top down as I did so. The zip on my skirt was half-undone; before anyone could see it I wrapped my jumper round my middle and tied it at the front. Just moving stirred the sickness up in waves and I put one hand on my stomach, hidden under the knotted arms of my jumper. My tummy felt tender and bloated; gently I rubbed at it, wishing my skirt wasn't so tight. I wriggled my hand round under the jumper and pulled my zip down a little further, keeping my hand over it so no one would see.

I still felt hot and so *sick*. My clothes seemed to be sticking to me and under my hair the back of my neck felt clammy. I leant over my work, one arm crossed over my middle, holding on to my zip, and the other resting my elbow on the desk, hand propping up my head, pushing the damp hair away from my neck. I stayed like that for ages; if I didn't move the sickness eased back just a little, but then Mrs Blackmore said, 'Are you going to do any work today, Kate?' and I had to turn the page, move my pen about, pretend I was getting on.

I needed to go to the loo, needed to go quite badly. That and trying to swallow down the nausea was making me hotter, making me sweat. Yet when the bell eventually went I had to wait till everyone else left the classroom before I could get up. I pretended to sort out my books until Mrs Blackmore had gone and everyone else too, then I could sort out my clothes, do my zip back up as far as it would go, put my jumper back on, and get my body hidden again.

Standing up caused the sickness to rush up again. The Maths room was near the main loos; I grabbed up my stuff and rushed out the class, and just made it downstairs to the loos and into a cubicle before I threw up, down into the dirty pan. Threw up not much, just liquid and dribble mostly, but still I retched and retched and each time I did so I breathed in great gulpfuls of the horrible stink of it, of vomit, mixed with all the other foul smells, acid in my mouth and my nose.

When it was all out I still stood there, bent over the loo, trying to slow my breath. Puking makes your eyes water, and I was crying. I yanked off sheets of crunchy hard toilet roll and scratched it over my face, over my eyes and my mouth, but it did no good so I wiped my face on my jumper and flushed the paper away. And then the cramps came, ripping across my middle, and I could barely get my knickers down quick enough; I sat on the hard cold loo seat while the flush was still churning and stayed like that, bent double over my knees while the pain gripped and twisted.

It came in waves. I couldn't even breathe except in short, tight bursts. Vaguely I could hear voices outside the door, voices whispering, giggling, but I didn't care;

couldn't care about anything but this *pain*, wrenching me out.

'Jesus, what a fucking stink!' someone said and they were right outside the door, banging on it.

'Who's in there?' said another.

'Kid from Year Ten,' someone replied. 'Don't want her running out of bog roll. Better make sure she's all right.'

Then over the top came a loo roll, hitting me on the head and unravelling over my knees on to the floor. In the cubicle next door there was scuffling, then from above me a voice called, 'You all right in there, kid?' But I couldn't lift my head, couldn't even care that someone was staring down over the cubicle wall at me, seeing me sat there like that, with my knickers round my knees.

Then the person was gone again, back at ground level; I knew that because I could hear them talking about me through the door again instead of from above. 'Gut rot,' they said. 'Jesus, give us a fucking fag to kill the stink.'

'Who is it?' someone asked and I heard the strike and the hiss of a match as cigarettes were lit.

'Don't know her name. Girl that was going out with Glenn Williams. You know, skinny girl with the dark brown hair. God, what a stink.'

And so they went on. I sat there till they were gone. I sat there till there was silence, then I picked the toilet paper up off the floor and tore it up into wodges to make it as soft as I could. Gently I wiped at myself; there was blood, I knew there would be. Not much, but blood nonetheless, crimson-bright in the gloom. I wiped it away as best as I could then I pressed the handle, but the cistern spluttered and would not flush. I pressed it again; nothing. My legs were numb from sitting so long. I unlocked the cubicle, leaving the toilet heaped with spirals of hard, stained paper.

On jelly legs I walked round to the sinks and leant against the edge while the tap ran ice-cold. I put my hands into the water, then cupped them together and splashed at my face. There was no soap of course. I looked up at the wall above the sink where it said *Sara Williams is a slag* and all those other things; underneath all that someone had added more, someone had written *Sara Williams has got margarine legs* and under that *Sara Williams fucks for fags*. While I leant against the sink, reading this, someone else came in; I saw her in the mirror, a fat girl from the first year.

It was lesson time now; apart from her I was alone. I listened to her pee noisily, the scrunch of hard paper, the half-hearted attempt to flush the loo, then out she went. When I was alone again, I got a pen out from my bag and scratched out all the horrible things written about me, scratched out *So is Kate Harper*, scratched out *Hear, hear*. I should have done it before. I shouldn't have left it there till now that I was sick as a pig, sick, *sick*.

I left all the things about Sara. I left them all there for everyone to see and I read them, over and over, thinking *Good, good, good* while I felt the stickiness in my knickers, thickening, wet at the tops of my thighs.

It was just like a period, I told myself and I felt detached, like in a moment of crisis, or disaster. Some other force was taking over, some other me was thinking *What shall I do? What shall I do?* I went back into a cubicle, a different one this time, and sat down again on the toilet; my knickers were soaked red. I saw this and started to shake, my teeth chattering. I tore off reams of toilet paper, folding it up carefully, neatly, padding it between my legs. It was horrible, hard paper, and it soaked up nothing; it slid wet inside my knickers as I walked out of the loos and out of the school, and headed for home.

It was a half-hour walk home normally and I was walking slowly now. The toilet paper was sticking to me where some of the blood had dried and it was catching on my skin. But I couldn't try to move it at all, I didn't dare; the bleeding wasn't stopping, I could feel it hot and thick, filling up inside my clothes. It was probably soaking into my skirt at the back and I'd left my jacket at school; I'd got nothing to hide it, soon everyone would be able to see, but I couldn't walk any faster. I couldn't walk any faster because if I did it would start spilling out everywhere.

It'd stopped hurting now; now I could feel nothing except the wetness on my thighs, and by the time I got home there were red beads running down my legs, smudging at my knees. No one was home. As I closed the front door behind me and kicked off my shoes a red drop hit the carpet. I did not know whether to go into the bathroom or to my bedroom; then the pain came back, slicing across my stomach, pulling me down. I did not know what to do.

The bathroom was nearest. I sat on the loo, fully dressed; it wasn't just pain now but a pushing, pushing feeling, like being pulled inside out. I was soaked; my knickers, my thighs, the back of my skirt. I knew I ought to take my things off but I couldn't; I was such a mess that I was afraid to leave the loo, but I needed to lie down. I got off the loo and climbed into the bath; there was red smeared all up the side, red on my hands, my legs. I lay back in the bath and felt my body pushing down. I pressed my skirt between my legs, and tried to contain what was happening, tried to soak it up, to stop it. But at the same time as I was shoving the material of my skirt down over myself I was also starting to pull down my knickers because it was coming out, whatever I did it was coming out.

I didn't know what time it was, but it was a Tuesday,

and my mum always gets home about sixish on a Tuesday and my dad right after her. She found me first, pushing out chopped liver and screaming from the pain.

'Oh my dear Lord!' she cried. Then she was right there with her hands in the mess, yelling at my dad who was just behind her, struck stupid in the doorway. 'Get an ambulance, Tony. Quick! Get an *ambulance!*'

They didn't though. In the end there wasn't time. My mum told my dad to bring all the towels from the airing cupboard and they piled me and the towels into the car and drove me to the hospital. My dad carried me into A&E; I saw his face, appalled as I bled into his arms.

It was hanging out of me. I felt it wobble against my thighs as I was slapped on to the bed. A blanket was thrown across me, my arm yanked out, my inner wrist rubbed and a line shot in.

I could feel it hanging out. I leant forward, I tried to see it, but they pushed me back down on to the bed, held me there, and started counting me out.

23

I was floating.

Someone had stuffed a huge sanitary towel between my thighs; I moved my legs slightly and I could feel it, big and soft, like when I was little, and used to curl up in bed and shove my pillow there for comfort. I could move my legs, and my fingers slightly too, I could waggle them and feel the blanket underneath them, all soft holes. Like a baby blanket, tucked up cosy around me. I could move my arms too, if I could be bothered; I could turn my head too, probably, if I tried.

I could open my eyes, if I wanted to. Or I could just stay like that forever, floating.

Something was annoying my wrist. I wanted to move my hand, to touch it with the other hand, to open my eyes, look, and sort it out. The hand with the sore wrist twitched involuntarily; I couldn't stop it. I screwed up my face, eyes held tightly shut, desperately trying to hold on to oblivion, but I heard a chair scrape beside me and I heard my dad's voice, saying something, just one word. *What* or *Nurse* or *Kate* or something. Then there were cold fingers on my hand, doing something to my wrist, and some other voice, a female voice, murmured something I didn't quite catch and then—

'Ouch!'

I tried to yank back my hand, but I couldn't. I opened my eyes and light sliced cold, sharp into my head.

The nurse pulling the line out of my wrist said, 'Ssh, ssh, just a little tug that's all . . . there, done.' She kept hold of my hand and rubbed it between her own. 'All over now, dear,' she said. 'You're back with us now.'

I wished she would let go of my hand. I wished she would go away and I could close my eyes again and curl back into the dark.

'Someone's here for you.' She nodded to where my dad was, as if I didn't know he was there. 'Someone's been waiting a long time for you to wake up.' She looked back at me, eyebrows raised, smiling expectantly like I might turn to him and say *Dad! Great to see you!*

I didn't turn my head; I didn't want to see him at all, but then he was there anyway, beside the nurse, and – oh God, oh God, I couldn't bear to see his face, his stunned, greyed-out face . . .

I started crying then, fat tears running sideways into my hair, and it hurt my stomach, crying. Hurt deep inside where I was raw, stripped bare.

My dad held both my hands in his while I cried and

cried. 'Kate, oh Kate, oh Kate,' he said, over and over, like there were no other words.

My dad was still holding my hand when my mum came in, but he let it go when he heard the door open, and stood up, away from me. 'She's awake now,' he told her, but he didn't sound very happy about it.

My mum looked at me but said nothing; for just a second our eyes met, then she looked away again and started emptying her bag. She'd brought me a bottle of Ribena; she put it on top of the bedside cupboard next to the water jug and the throw-away sick bowls. I remembered, and I knew she must have done too, another time, so similar and yet so different when I was about eight or so and spent a night in hospital to have a cyst removed from my ear. She brought me Ribena that time too. She knew it was my favourite and we never had it at home. It was for special occasions only, Ribena.

She'd brought me my pyjamas too, and a towel and my tooth brush. When she opened the cupboard to put them inside the room filled up with the smell of old orange peel.

But there were no chocolates, there were no flowers.

There were no smiles for the big brave girl this time.

'What was it? What was it?' I asked them, but they wouldn't tell me.

'Hush, hush,' the nurse said. 'You get some rest now,' but I wouldn't hush, hush, I wanted to know, I *had* to know.

She took the blood-pressure band off my arm and I grabbed her hand. I wouldn't let her go. 'What was it?' I asked again and I shook her, holding on to her arm with both hands now; I would not let her go. 'What was it?' I said, but I felt that she couldn't hear me, no one could hear me, so next time I screamed it: '*What was it?*'

'Kate!' barked my dad, but I wouldn't let go my grip.

The nurse called out, 'Doctor!' and pressed the button over my bed, taking me with her, clinging on. The doctor came running in ready for an emergency but there was none, there was just me, screaming and clinging, screaming and clinging. His white coat, his cold face; they acted on me like a slap. I paused for a moment and they looked at each other, the doctor, the nurse, my dad.

'Tell me!' I screamed again. 'Tell me!'

The doctor pushed his glasses up on his nose. 'It was too early to tell,' he said but I wasn't having that. I knew he was lying. I was kneeling now, up on the bed; the wire from my arm snapped free of the drip and, now that I had let her go, the nurse started busying herself, re-tying wires to tubes, tubes to wires.

'What was it?' I yelled again. 'For God's sake just tell me! Please! I have to know!'

And so he told me.

It was a girl.

Of course, it was a girl.

24

They kept me in hospital for four days because of the bleeding. At first I wasn't even allowed up; not even to pee. They stuck a catheter in me and rigged up a horrible little bag by the side of the bed. Every few hours someone would come round, pull off my covers, check the catheter, check the bleeding, check the stitches where they'd had to widen me up to get their tools in.

They said I was lucky there was no permanent damage. They said I was lucky they'd got it all out that way and hadn't had to cut my stomach open. There was no reason why I couldn't go on to have healthy children, the doctor said, one day, one far-off day.

Lucky, lucky me.

They didn't tell me that my body would still think itself pregnant. They didn't tell me that my breasts would still be sore, more so than before because now there were confused messages going on in my poor little brain. My breasts ached, they felt hot and heavy. I rubbed them with my hand to try and soothe the pain but the pain got worse, right behind the nipples, then out in came, not much but out it came, thin, yellow milk running warm over my hand.

* * *

On the third day, when they'd taken out the catheter and were *hmming* and *haaing* about letting me go home, a social worker came to see me. The hospital must have called her. They must have phoned Social Services, and said *We've got another pregnant teenager in.*

My parents sure as hell didn't want her there. My parents stood back from my bed, mortified, *horrified*, while she reeled off her questions: did I know what had happened, did I understand, did I understand it was against the law for minors to have *sex*, sordid, sordid *sex*; was I coerced, abused; was he older, younger, did I know who it was, the father of my poor dead baby?

I stared at my parents, they stared at me; my mum gripped my dad's arm, sobbed, choked on it and put her hand to her mouth.

This was real, this was the dirt; did I even know who he was, the father of my poor dead baby?

She went away with her questions unanswered, saying I should think about it, saying she'd be back – *in touch* was how she put it. Oh she *so* wanted to know who the father was. She held my gaze, long, intent, like she'd held the gaze of a thousand stupid, teenage tarts, and said she was sure my parents would want to know too.

But until then they *hadn't*. Until then they'd been too shocked, I suppose. My dad had just been there, by my side, like it was an illness I'd got, and my mum had come and gone, bringing what I needed – more pyjamas, knickers, enormous great sanitary towels – saying nothing much at all.

But that witch of a social worker had snapped them out of their shock and put the wind of revenge up them, and my God they wanted to know. *Who was it? Who was it?* Whispered at first, at the hospital where anyone could hear, but at home, when I was supposed to be resting still, the tempo rose and it was *Who was it? Who was it?* shouted into my face.

But to me it was absurd that they even needed to ask. Absurd, *hateful*, that anyone, never mind some bitch of a stranger, never mind my own *parents*, could think that I would have to rack my brains and think about that one. Could think that there might be so many blokes I've let screw me that I wouldn't know who it was without *thinking about it*.

I mean, who else could it be? Who else could they possibly think?

'Sara's *brother?*'

My dad tore at the air with his hands, ripping up the space between us as if his fingers were claws. '*Sara's brother?*'

Behind him my mother drew in her breath on a gasp. She looked stunned, felled, like an animal, shocked beyond feeling. I couldn't bear to see her face; I dropped my head back down into my arms, on to the arm of the sofa, where I was curled up, *resting*.

'*Sara's brother?*' he said again like it was curtain down, curtain up, like the lights should dim, we should exit, then come in again, ready for part two.

But there was no part two. There was only part one and its messy end. My mother was crying now, muttering *How could I be so stupid?* and *I should have known, I should have known* and my dad loomed over me, stuck in glue, ready to run, ready to pounce, going nowhere.

'Is that what you were doing?' he shouted at me. 'Is it? *Look at me when I am talking to you!*'

I raised my head and watched my dad slam his hands against invisible walls; he wrenched his body from side to side but his feet didn't move. His feet were stuck in glue.

'Is that what you were doing all those Saturday nights when I took you to their house? Is it? Is it? This is not the end.' His voice broke over the words; he pointed his finger at me and his hand was shaking. 'This is not the end,' he said again but he was wrong, so wrong.

It *was* the end.

I hid my head again and felt the fabric of the sofa, rough and wet against my cheek. I seemed to have been crying forever. I couldn't believe that I'd told them. I couldn't believe how easily it came out. I could see Sara

and Glenn and everything we ever were, everything I
ever wanted for us disappear now, dead, like our baby.

25

I was off school five weeks in all. When I came out of hospital I had to stay at home for another week, resting, and then it was the Easter holidays.

I phoned Sara's house, several times, but all I got was the dead tone, the no reply tone, the *no one can hear you* tone. She didn't have a mobile – well she did, but it didn't work, nor did Glenn's. They couldn't afford the bills. Suddenly a picture flashed into my head of their feet stamping on ten-pound notes, abortion money, murder money.

It wasn't even needed in the end.

I still had this stupid, frantic notion that Sara and I could somehow become friends again. I just could not let her go. So I wrote her a letter, a desperate, desperate letter. I totally poured out my heart. I told her I'd only ever wanted to be with her and that I'd give anything to go back to how we were, in the beginning.

And I told her our baby was dead. *Our* baby. Of course my dad must already have told her, or told Glenn at least, with very different words, but I wrote *Our baby is dead, Sara, don't let it mean that we are too.*

And as soon as I was allowed out, as soon as I could

go anywhere without bleeding half to death, I walked to the little post office round the corner from us, bought a stamp and stuck my letter in the box. I do not know if she ever received it.

In our house there was a very *hushed* atmosphere.

Since that outburst when I'd told them the baby was Glenn's my parents had not said a thing more about it, to me. They must have done something about it, they must have said something, to someone, to Glenn, to Glenn's parents, to the school . . . I don't know. They never said anything else about it to me at all.

I guess they must have thought what had happened was punishment enough in itself.

They just came and went as usual, and mostly in those few weeks I lay on the sofa or stayed in my room. They spoke to each other, as normal, about other things. And they talked to me, a bit, in that quiet way, that polite way, like nothing had happened, but it had, we all knew that it had.

I suppose they wanted us all to put it behind us. As if I ever could.

I told them at school I'd had glandular fever. It was my mum's idea. The Monday I went back she dropped me off in the car and I panicked.

'I can't go in,' I said, 'I can't.'

'Tell them you've had glandular fever,' my mum said. 'That's all they need to know.'

So I did. I said it so often I started believing it myself.

It was the weirdest thing going back through those gates and walking across the playground. I thought everyone would be staring at me. The bell had already gone and lots of people had started going in; I joined the rest, shuffling up the stairs to tutorial. It was so, so strange. Like even though this terrible, terrible thing had happened, suddenly I was back where I was before, thinking of nothing except seeing Sara again.

I walked into tutorial and my eyes homed straight in to where Sara sat; she wasn't there. Disappointment and relief clashed inside me; a temporary reprieve. Mrs Rupert never called our names out; she sat there with the register open and scanned the class, ticking off our names while we got on with some work, supposedly. I saw her eyes flick around the room, over me, over the empty space beside me.

I sat through the whole of tutorial waiting for Sara to come in late. She didn't. All day, she didn't come.

Next day she still wasn't there and I missed her more now that I was back at school than I had at home. At home I'd been in limbo, in a sort of non-time; head thick, body slow. Shock, I suppose, numbing me up.

I had to speak to her. Oh I was prepared for her fury but I had to speak to her. I had to know that she *knew*.

I had to see her face, see her eyes when I told her *Our baby is dead*.

Wednesday she didn't come and by now I was afraid. I noticed in Biology that there was no longer a seat for her. We sat in rows in Biology, all facing the front. There was no space to show that Sara was missing; everyone had moved along and closed up the gap.

After school I walked past her house; there were no bikes outside, no sign of life, but that didn't mean they weren't in there. It wasn't dark enough yet for the lights to be on and how else could I tell? I crept up the side path, just a few steps. I thought I might see something through the glass of the kitchen door, shadows, steam on the kitchen window, *something*.

You can tell when a house is empty.

Fear turned in my stomach, spreading down into my thighs.

I walked a few steps up the road, sat on a wall opposite their house, and *waited* for them to come home. I checked my watch; four o'clock passed, and half-past four, and no one came. Maybe someone *was* inside; I watched for a light to come on. You needed to put the lights on pretty early in that house, it was so gloomy inside. I was panicking now but I couldn't give up. I pulled up the collar of my jumper, stuffed it into my mouth, and bit on it to still my teeth. I rocked my body to chase off the fear and the cold. I told myself over and over *She will be there, she will be there.*

I heard footsteps coming along the street. Heard them but took no notice; they weren't Sara's footsteps, I would have known if they were Sara's footsteps. So I didn't even look up, not until the footsteps came closer, and slowed down.

'What are *you* doing here?'

Now I glanced up and it was like providence; it was Rachel in gold-and-blue blazer, coming home from St Mary's.

'Rachel!' I cried and I was so, so pleased to see her, but Rachel was frowning, Rachel was saying things I couldn't bear to hear.

'They're not there,' she said. 'They've gone. Moved out. *Gone.*'

I stared at her. It couldn't be true.

'They can't have just gone!' Panic made my voice shrill. Rachel moved to carry on walking by but I grabbed her arm, stopping her. '*Where* have they gone?'

'*Away.*' Rachel shook off my arm, and pushed past me.

'Where?' I followed her down the street, calling after her. '*Where? Give me their address. Where* have they gone? *Tell* me!'

Outside her house Rachel stopped, pushed open the gateway then closed it behind her. Leaning over the gate she half-whispered so no one in the house could hear, 'No I won't tell you. Now just shut up and go away.

They've *gone*.' She started walking up the pathway to her door then she stopped and turned around again. 'What else did you expect?' she said. 'What else could they do? Glenn was kicked out of *school* because of you!'

I waited for Sara to come back.

Constantly I waited, constantly I looked out for her. I was convinced I'd see her again. Sometimes I'd be out in the street and I'd get this feeling that she was there behind me and I'd turn round expecting to see her. The hairs on the back of my neck would rise and my skin would tighten with the conviction, the *desire*, that she'd be there, my Sara, my Sara.

I wrote a letter to Rachel, pleading with her to give me Sara's new address. She didn't reply, so I waited near her house one day to catch her on her way home from school again.

'Don't you think you've done enough harm?' she said. 'Just go away.'

But still I couldn't give up. I'd walk down her road, wishing upon wish that she'd be there, at last she'd be there, walking up the street just like she used to, shoulders hunched as if the sunshine was cold on her body, head bent, arms folded across her heart.

For ages their house stood empty. I walked past it every day on my way home from school, torturing myself.

Then one day there was a car parked outside, the leaves had all been swept off the path, and the cobwebs cleaned away from the front door.

It wasn't their house any more. Their things were gone from inside; their voices gone forever.

I read in a book once that there is a path mapped out for every one of us. And when we reach the end of that path we die, and our souls disappear into the atmosphere like tiny pieces of one vast spiritual mosaic, each in its place.

It kind of made sense when I read it but now I wonder, what happens if you die before you're born? What happens to you then?

What about my baby, who everyone wants to forget? Where is she?

My parents never talk about it because that's not the way things are done in our house. In our house you don't dwell on things, you move on.

And I never speak about it to them because what could I say? How could I explain that it was Sara I loved, not Glenn? How would they ever understand that?

I had masses of work to do, to make up for all the time I'd missed off school. I threw myself into it. There was nothing else to do. And it took my mind off things, a little.

I focused on the future, on going off to college and

university, and getting away. I couldn't wait to get away, from the stuck-in-the-past superciliousness of Juliet and co, and from everything that I'd lost.

And so you do move on. You have to in the end.

You move on, but you don't forget. You take what's happened with you. It sticks, like a rotten old nut, deep down inside.